Merry Misfits

HOUSE OF MISFITS

CAMBRIA HEBERT

Merry
Misfits

HOUSE OF MISFITS
CAMBRIA HEBERT

Experience the magic of New York City at Christmas with
Fletcher and the rest of the misfit family as they create
family traditions and memories through special dates and
holiday fun.

Be prepared for lots of fluff, laughter, grumbling grumps,
swoony romance, and surprises!

Merry Misfits is a special House of Misfits holiday novella
featuring the entire misfit family

and is told in alternating POVs of some of your favorites.
This novella features both male/female and male/male
couples.

Merry Misfits is approximately 48,000 words and is book
five in the series.

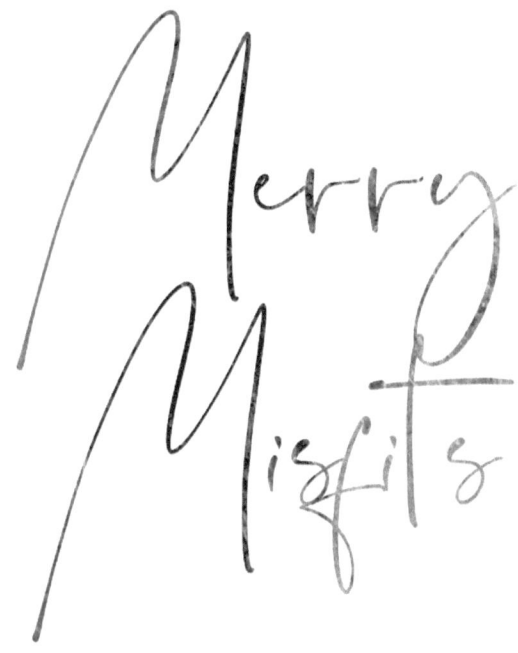

HOUSE OF MISFITS

CAMBRIA HEBERT

ONE UPON A TIME

Spider-Man wore a Santa hat and eggnog ruined a surprise.

1

GRINCH

THE MOST WONDERFUL TIME OF THE YEAR MY ASS.

You know what December in New York City was like? It was like getting a root canal from a dentist who was half blind, had shaky hands, and didn't use any kind of numbing agent.

In short, it sucked.

Damn holidays.

And they were endless. October was barely over when all the hustle and bustle started 'round here. Between the massive light displays, window decorations, and people running from one shop to another, I could barely walk down the street without getting annoyed.

Then there was the Thanksgiving Day parade, the turkey day itself, and then even more holiday crap people thought was festive. What the hell did New York need a giant tree for?

We didn't.

But we got one anyway, along with the bitter cold and snow everyone thought was just *so charming.* All it did was create more traffic and a mess of the roads.

I couldn't wait until Christmas was over. I couldn't wait for people to go back to their regularly scheduled grumpiness instead of their cheer, which actually just made them grumpier.

That's why I didn't even pretend to be all happy and jolly. Someone around here had to keep a level head anyway, and clearly, I was the only one capable.

I didn't need Christmas. What was the point?

All it did was create extra madness and work…

And maybe a little extra loneliness.

2

"No."

A moment of loud silence followed the absolute resolve in the single word Ethan dropped into this conversation. If you could even call it that. It was more like him telling me what to do.

"But, E!" I whined. I wasn't above it. It usually worked. "I do it every year!"

I hoped he wouldn't call me out by pointing out "every year" was actually only the last two years. But still, I liked those two times!

Instead, all he did was shake his blond head once and cross his impressively toned arms over his chest. I couldn't help it. My eyes strayed to the action, momentarily forgetting I was supposed to be arguing. It was hard to argue with someone who looked like a walking Avenger all the time.

When I finally forced my eyes back up, there was a

knowing glint in his. My chin jutted out. *He better not bring that up either!*

"This year is different," was all he said.

"Why?"

"Because you have me."

My heart tumbled a bit, and the annoyance I felt completely melted away. A soft noise escaped my throat, and everything about him softened. Opening his arms, he motioned for me.

"Come here."

Hurrying across the room, I leaped into his waiting arms, legs locking around his waist, arms looping around his neck.

"My good boy," he whispered softly, dipping his head to capture my lips.

Parting my lips instantly, my tongue anticipated his, and the minute it stroked over mine, I sighed, settling farther into his chest. Tongues dancing, Ethan carried me to the couch to sit, my legs still wrapped around his middle.

His large, warm palm stroked up my back until strong, skillful fingers wrapped around the back of my neck. I shivered under his strength, opening a little wider, asking him to come just a little bit deeper.

The second he did, I arched into his wide frame, my hips automatically bearing down on his lap. A low sound vibrated his throat, and it added an extra texture to the already brain-fogging kiss. It was so easy to forget words, thoughts… an entire conversation when his mouth locked with mine.

We kissed until my lungs burned, desperate for air, but still, I didn't want to pull away. Pausing mid-kiss, I sucked in a deep breath, moving against him anew as the scent of cinnamon and pine swirled around us.

His tongue chased mine when I started to pull back, a growl rumbling deep in Ethan's throat. The fingers wrapped around the back of my neck dug in, sending delicious waves through my lower half.

Oh, I loved his dominance. I loved giving in to him, letting him take total control.

Not of this, Fletcher. Not of this.

The thought made me pull back, but I didn't go far. The wide hand against my back saw to that. I scowled despite the pleasure thrumming through my veins. "You're trying to distract me."

"Maybe at first." E allowed, but when his deep-blue eyes met mine, I saw the hunger. "But then I forgot what I was doing as I always do when you melt for me."

I swayed closer, the heat of his body so enticing. His lips parted, and I almost gave in.

"I'm working at the tree stand. I already promised him I'd be there," I said, mutinous.

"Him who?" Ethan glowered, eyes narrowing into small slits.

"Old Mr. Holly," I replied, rolling my eyes at his obvious jealousy. *Like anyone could ever be better than him.* "The man who owns the stand."

Ethan grunted in response. But then his gaze turned speculative. "How old is old?"

I laughed. "It doesn't matter. I only love you."

Everything about him softened, his stare turned into a caress, and my stomach felt funny as he smiled. "I love you too, puppy."

I leaned in for another kiss, but Ethan spoke, his lips nearly brushing mine with every word. "I still want to know."

A strangled sound ripped from me, and I pushed off

his chest to sit back. "Old enough to be my grandpa. He needs help, E. I'm going."

"You can't just work on the streets in the Grimms."

"I do every year!"

"That was before you became Upper East Side royalty."

I groaned. "But I'm still me."

His hand cupped my face. Automatically, I pushed my cheek farther into his palm. "I know that. But you're well known now. You can't just go around in the ghetto like before. It's not safe."

Agitated, I climbed out of Ethan's lap, nearly pitching sideways onto the floor in my haste.

He caught me with gentle hands and a low sound falling between us. "Careful." He cautioned, holding on to me as I continued to scramble away. His hands didn't pull back until I was firmly on my feet, and the sweetness of that gesture made me feel a little guilty for arguing.

Just climb back into his lap and kiss him again. Oh, how tempting those taunting thoughts were.

But I couldn't. This was important to me. When I spun away, my eyes fell on a stack of colorfully wrapped gifts, all of them with elaborate bows and tags. All of them from our fans and various designers and all of them waiting to be placed under the main live tree we had yet to get.

I'd never seen so many gifts before. And they weren't even from our family. I never even got Christmas presents until I moved in with my brothers, and even then, we only did simple things. This was overwhelming, and as grateful as I was, it made me want to cling to something familiar even more.

"Fletch." Ethan's soft voice beckoned, and I turned.

My lower lip wobbled. "It's my tradition!" I burst out. "My whole life, I never had a tree. *She* never let us celebrate. But then one year, Mr. Holly let me work at his tree stand. So many trees, and they smelled so good! When it snowed, it would cling on their branches. People would come and wander under the lights draped around, and they would smile and be so happy to pick one. We had roasted chestnuts and hot chocolate." I felt my shoulders slump. "It was nice, even if it is the ghetto."

Hauling me close, Ethan locked his arms around me with a low sound. His face buried itself in my hair, and I felt him inhale. "I wish I could make up for every Christmas you were denied."

"That's not what I'm asking for." I sniffled into his shirt, rubbing my nose against its softness. "I just want you to understand." Lifting my face, I confessed. "I know I missed out on a whole lot. I know where I am now is a lot different than where I was. But not all of it was bad. Some of it was good. It was mine. I know it probably sounds stupid—"

"Nothing you say can ever sound stupid," Ethan insisted, giving me a squeeze to punctuate his words.

"I found Christmas there. I don't want to leave it behind."

"How about I just buy you your own tree stand?"

"E!" I groaned, which I used to stifle my giggle.

"An entire tree farm upstate?" he pondered.

This time I couldn't hide my laugh. "Richie."

His chuckle was warm, melting over me the way marshmallows turned soft in hot chocolate.

"I'm joking," he told me as if I didn't know. Running a hand down the length of my back, his palm settled at the base of my spine. "When do you start?"

I pulled back, still holding his waist. "Really?"

His face softened, his smile so genuine his dimple showed. "I would never ask you to turn away from something that means so much to you."

He barely rocked onto his heels when I flung myself against him, squeezing tight. "Thank you, E!"

I didn't need Ethan's permission to work there. Or anywhere. I didn't need his permission to do anything at all. But I wanted it. He was my safe place. My true home. Doing something he was against would hurt me just as much as it would him.

"Hey." His voice was soft, and the little bit of playfulness from before disappeared. His hands swallowed up my face when he cupped the sides. The feel of his fingertips in the hair around my ears tickled with familiarity.

The azure shade of his eyes was sincere and shining as it settled wholly on me. "Thank you for telling me this. It means so much to me when you share pieces of the time when I wasn't there."

I knew he wondered a lot about my childhood, what it was like growing up with *her*. He worried a lot about all the stuff I missed out on. "Don't be upset, E," I implored, laying my palm against his cheek. "In all honesty, the things I never had probably bother you more than they do me."

He frowned.

"I couldn't feel the loss of something I never had," I explained.

"But what about when you found it? At the tree stand? With your brothers?"

"With you," I added.

Pulling away, he paced toward the wall of windows that framed a perfect view of a frosted city. I could look out these windows every day for the rest of my life, but I would always find something new to see.

"Is all of this," he said, sweeping his arm around our fully decked-out penthouse, "too much? Is it—" He stopped speaking for a minute before clearing his throat. "Painful for you?"

His back was to me, his sculpted, broad shoulders tense against the city backdrop. I nearly tripped rushing to him, throwing my arms around his waist to press my cheek against his back.

"No! It's not. I swear! I love it. I'm pretty sure we have more decorations than Macy's!"

Ethan made a sound. "They should hire a new design team."

Glancing around, I smiled. The turkey was barely cool from Thanksgiving, and Ethan had a whole team of people here to turn the entire penthouse into some Christmas extravaganza. I'd never seen so many ornaments, greenery, and glitter. There was even a big tree made out of poinsettias in the foyer the elevator opened up into before we even came in the front door.

We had another tree in the foyer inside the apartment too. It was the first thing you saw when you came inside, and it was twelve feet tall. And Marvel-themed! It occupied the space where we usually had a table with my statue of Spider-Man, so when the table got moved out and the tree came in, we decided to fill it up with Marvel ornaments.

Ethan's designers were horrified.

He told them to worry about the other stuff, and we did the tree ourselves. We even positioned Spidey so it looked like he was shooting tinsel (instead of webs) out of his wrists at the tree. And I got him a Santa hat, making him Spidey Santa.

It was pretty epic.

Turning in my arms, Ethan slid his around mine and

sighed. "I wanted to give you a good Christmas. I never meant to overwhelm you or remind you of things you didn't have."

Pulling away, he paced more. I knew he was upset because of the pacing.

"I went overboard."

"You decorate every year," I pointed out.

His strides faltered with his grimace. "Well, maybe I did a little extra this year."

I couldn't help it. My heart swelled up, making my ribcage feel tight. "For me?"

"Always for you."

I made the sound that had almost become a calling card. A sound I always made when I wanted him.

He came, of course. He always did.

I exhaled the minute I came up against his chest, nuzzling into the side of his throat. Looping my arms around his neck, I smiled. "I love the decorations and that we did some of it together. I love that you took off work yesterday so we could make cookies."

He groaned. "*Attempted* to make cookies."

"They tasted great!" I insisted. Okay, I didn't insist. I just lied.

"Have you been eating them?" Horrified, he pulled back to look me over. "I told you not to eat them. Great gods, you're going to get sick!"

I turned sheepish. "I tried to eat one this morning before you came downstairs." I wrinkled my nose and confessed. "I guess they really aren't very good."

He threw back his head and laughed. "We should have thrown them away."

"No!" I insisted. "We made them together. They're the best cookies I've ever had. Even if they are hard as a rock and a weird brown color."

He laughed again.

My chin jutted out. "I'm not joking."

He made a soft cajoling sound, a smile still playing around his lips. "I know, love. They're my favorite too. But maybe don't eat them, okay? Jane can help us make edible ones this weekend."

I nodded. "Ethan?"

"Anything," he echoed.

"Please don't be upset about what I said. I didn't mean to make you feel bad. Being here with you could never be painful. Everything you do for me only reminds me how much you love me."

Leaning in, he kissed me lightly, licking over my lower lip before pulling back. "I do love you, Fletch. So much. And you didn't make me feel bad, so never be afraid to share anything with me. I'll always listen and try to understand. All I want is for you to be happy. I know I tend to be a bit overzealous when it comes to you—"

Meow! Gwennie appeared, making her presence known and rubbing along my ankle before looping around one of Ethan's.

I glanced down and laughed. She had red tinsel on her back and a silver icicle stuck to her tail. She liked the Marvel tree as much as I did.

"My God, we will be finding that stuff all over this apartment until next year!" Ethan groaned.

"I hope so." I snickered.

"I apologize for being so—" he said, pausing while his big brain searched for a word.

"Overprotective?" I supplied.

"Adamant." He corrected. I pursed my lips, making him sigh. "I just worry."

"I can take care of myself," I insisted. "But I appreciate

you worrying about me."

"So when does this, ah, job begin?"

"Tomorrow."

He gasped. Sometimes he was very dramatic. "Tomorrow! It's too soon."

"For what?" I wondered. "It's December, so it's not too early for people to come get a real tree."

"I have to work."

"So do I," I insisted.

"How long does this tree stand stay open?"

"Until we run out of trees."

His eyes turned speculative.

Crossing my arms over my chest, I told him, "Don't even think about coming down there and buying them all."

"Wouldn't dream of it," he murmured.

He was totally dreaming of it.

Finally, he relented. "If anyone gives you a hard time, you'll come home. Agreed?"

"No one will give me any trouble."

"Fletcher." The warning in his tone made me want to instantly obey.

Despite it, I said, "I won't come home."

Ethan's sharp intake of breath made my heart rate spike. "What did you just say?" he nearly growled.

His narrowed, glittering eyes watched as I came closer, reaching out to curl a hand around the pink tie at his neck. Caressing the silk while looking up from beneath my lashes, I replied, "I won't come home if I have trouble. I'll come find you instead."

His nostrils flared, and the poised Upper East Side prince lost composure as desire took over. "Are you teasing me?"

I let the tie fall back against his chest. My ears grew

warm, and I could already hear the blood hammering through my veins. "And if I am?"

He started walking, backing me up until my legs hit the couch. Even still, he kept advancing, pushing me into the oversized cushions to cage me in with his entire body. "Then I'll have to retaliate."

A little whine slipped from between my lips as I arched up toward him. He stayed rigid, not letting me mold against him.

I was already buzzing with desire, already desperate to have his hands on me. I used his strong shoulders to pull myself up so my lips could brush against his ear. "Please, *daddy*."

That one word was all it took. Whatever was left of his composure snapped.

3

ETHAN

OH, THIS ONE.

There was only one person on this earth who could rile me up and push me over the edge. One man who could stubbornly argue one moment, have tears shimmering in his honey-colored gaze the next, and then turn me inside out with need. I was in a constant altering state of wanting to hand him the world on a silver platter, protect him at all costs, and do very, very naughty things to him.

Currently? It was totally the third.

Clearly, it was exactly what he wanted as he riled me up *and* called me daddy. He knew exactly what that word did to me.

I unwrapped his body like it was a gift I'd been given on Christmas morning. A gift I'd been dying to receive. Clothes flung over the side of the couch, and more littered the coffee table.

He was lean and long, his shoulders and arms defined from all the violin he played. Golden hair fell over his forehead, and his pupils were already blown wide. The sound of his heavy breathing excited me, as did the way his bare chest rapidly rose and fell.

Feeling starved, I latched onto one pink nipple to suck deep. He arched up, making a throaty sound, his hands fisting in my hair, holding me to him, something I allowed for long minutes because having his hands on me was something I loved.

When both nipples were swollen and sensitive, I dragged my teeth up to his collarbone, and he turned his head immediately. Smiling, I gave him another light bite and pulled away.

It took him a moment to realize I didn't give him what he wanted, and when he did, he whined, trying to grab me back. "Ethan."

"What?"

"You *know*…"

"And do you think I should just give you what you want after the way you teased?"

His hand curled around my tie and tugged. "Please."

"Please, what?"

"Please, daddy."

His little shivers spurred me on as I caressed the skin of his stomach, swirling around his belly button before delving down toward his cock, which was already standing at attention. A low sound hummed from his throat when I stroked over his swollen head, but it turned into a strangled sound when I pulled back faster than he wanted.

"No." I decided, moving to stand.

Pushing up onto his elbows, he stared at me, hunger and surprise glinting in his eyes. "Ethan?"

I started away, then heard him pushing up to follow. "Wait."

I turned back, pinning him with a stare. "Be a good boy. Stay there."

He nodded, lowering back to the couch, but when I started walking again, he made a sound of distress. It took everything I had to keep walking, to not run back and reassure him, but I kept going. Even still, when I stepped into the foyer, out of sight, I kept all my focus trained on him.

Opening the drawer of the console against the wall, I palmed the lube I always stashed there, then turned to grab something else as well.

He was still on the couch when I came back, but he was leaning up, eyes focused over the cushions in the direction in which I'd gone.

"I'm right here," I told him softly, unable to resist.

A brief flash of relief played over his features, and my chest swelled. Noticing what I had in my hands, his attention sharpened. "What are you doing?"

I smirked, straddling his legs with my knees. Holding up a long length of red tinsel, I smirked. "You mean with this?" I asked, drawing it lightly across his nipples, watching them tighten under the feathery caress. "You seem to like it when the cat drags this stuff all over, so I figured I would drag it all over you."

The shimmering red strands quivered with my movements as it feathered over his stomach on its way to his shaft. Impatient, he reached down to stroke himself.

"No," I told him, brushing his hand away.

His low whine tightened my dick and reminded me I was still fully clothed while he was completely bare. Taking the garland, I looped it around his dick, shimmying it lightly up and down the rigid length. He gasped and bucked up, reaching for himself, but I denied him again.

"Kiss me." He beckoned. Asking for the one thing I could never deny.

Before giving in, I looped the tinsel around the base of his shaft, tying it into a red, shining bow tight enough to cause sensation but not pain.

When it was done, I stroked the underside of his head, making him jolt. Sitting back, I admired my handiwork. "So pretty, my good boy. Do you feel like a present?"

Moving restlessly, he puckered his lips.

I growled, licking into him as our tongues swirled together. He kissed back greedily, arching into me and trying to rub his dick against my body. Without breaking the kiss, I reached between us to caress the inside of his thigh with the tail end of the garland. He shuddered, the kiss breaking with his moan.

Tugging it farther, I dragged it to the underside of his balls, letting its silky texture rub over his crack. His hands turned impatient, tugging my dress shirt out of my trousers to sink his fingers into my back.

I gave the bow a tug, making him pant. "Did I say you could touch me?"

"Please," he murmured, tugging again at my clothes.

Pulling back, I reached for another length of tinsel, using it to tie his wrists together and pinning them above his head.

"Ethan," he whined, wiggling his fingers. "Wanna touch you."

"This is your punishment for teasing me, puppy. Now just lie there and take whatever I give you."

He pouted. It was cute, and I almost gave in. Almost. "What do you say?"

"Yes, daddy."

My pants were uncomfortable, my dick straining against the fabric to get out, so I reached down and undid them, letting my throbbing cock breathe.

His eyes were already hazy as he watched me move.

"Fletcher." I beckoned, making him look up. "Remember your colors, love."

Not long after he figured out my, ah, daddy kink, I set up a color system for him. My inner alpha could be quite demanding, and while I knew he loved it, I always worried about going too far.

He nodded.

"What color are you?"

"Green."

"Green, what?"

"Green, *daddy*."

I kissed him softly before attacking. The sounds of lips smacking and moans rose to the ceiling as I worked his body thoroughly, holding back just enough.

His face would turn, offering up his neck every time I got close. I would deny the gesture, and every time, he would make a bereft plea.

Draping one of his legs over the back of the couch, I went to work, sucking across his inner thighs, leaving ownership marks in my wake.

"More." He squirmed, lowering his hands from above his head.

I bit down on his inner thigh, and he hissed a breath. "No."

His hands went back overhead, fingers sinking into the cushions as if that would keep them there. Smiling, I swirled my tongue around his hole, making his hips buck off the couch, pushing his body closer to my mouth. I chuckled, pinning him down with my forearm and licking over him again. And relentlessly again.

My name echoed around the apartment, and my chest tightened with love and possession. By the time I was done, he was panting and whining, the tip of his cock glistened, and his entrance was wet even as I was reaching for the lube.

Once my fingers were coated, I noted the way his shaft swelled around the tinsel, the bulbous head so flushed it nearly matched the decoration.

Dipping a finger beneath the place where it was tied, I smoothed some of the slippery lube around it. "Color," I demanded, worrying it had grown too tight.

"Green." He panted, lifting his hips.

"Hmm," I murmured, reaching down to tug the ends, making it tighten anew.

He moaned, shoulders coming up off the couch. Leaving it tight, I leaned down, swallowing his head, taking him until my lips hit the place I'd tied.

Forgetting his orders, he reached down, trying to free his hands.

I slipped a single digit into his body, making him forget about what he was doing as he wiggled around my finger, trying to get me to move. I denied the action, leaving my finger deep inside him, unmoving.

"*Please*, Ethan," he begged. "Please no more. Don't keep me away."

Just like that, I broke, thrusting my finger and tugging the tie around his cock free. He didn't even wait for me to free his hands, instead using his teeth to tug the bow away.

The tinsel was tossed aside, along with all of my clothes.

"Touch me," I invited. "Get as close as you can."

His legs twined around mine, pulling me in. Our tongues met, oddly not in a hurry, lazily dancing with the other, breaking free to explore every part we could reach before coming back to dance once more.

My skin buzzed with the high of finally having his hands on mine, of having his body sprawled out under me for the taking. We were both so keyed up it didn't take long for the kisses to turn fervent, our hips moving in sync as our erect cocks rubbed together, creating delicious friction.

"I'm ready." He panted, lifting his hips.

I didn't wait, thrusting into him with one push of my hips. Both of us groaned, my forehead falling onto the cushion above his shoulder.

Pulling back, I thrust back in, feeling Fletcher's nails curl into my skin. We moved and thrust in perfect sync, riding a wave of passion I'd only ever felt with him. I felt his body tighten, mine responding in turn.

"Ethan." He beckoned, dragging his fingers across my back.

Pulling up just enough so I could look into his blissed-out face, I couldn't help but smile. "What, love?"

"Will you give me what I want now?"

I smiled.

He turned his head, offering up his neck. And I nuzzled against it, thrusting into his core anew.

Arching up, he offered himself, and I latched on, sucking the love bite he wanted so much into the creamy skin of his neck.

The ones I'd left last time had faded, and he was offering up this part of himself for a fresh mark that would basically brand him when he went into the Grimms tomorrow.

I sucked a little deeper than probably necessary, and

the moment I did, he came apart beneath me. As if he'd been waiting to let go right at this moment.

Groaning, I eased up just a little as his release spilled between our bodies, marking us both. My lips went slack when I fell over the edge, spilling into his body, claiming him from the inside out.

Even after I'd come down, we both shook with little aftershocks, and I turned drowsy under the way he stroked and rubbed my back.

Finally, pushing up, I stared down through hazy vision. "I know we have this whole daddy kink thing between us, but I'd be a terrible dom."

His nose wrinkled. "Why?"

"Because I'm not strong enough to deny you very long."

His swollen lips stretched out into a beautiful smile. "But this is just enough for me."

I chuckled. "Of course it is because I'm so soft for you."

He kissed my cheek, and I melted all over again. Rolling off to the side, I pulled him into my chest, wrapping my body around his.

"I love you."

He echoed the same sweet words back to me.

"I'll never look at tinsel the same way again," he remarked.

I laughed. "Me either."

After a few quiet moments, I stroked over his hair. "Puppy?"

"Hmm?" he said, staying pressed into my chest.

"So Christmas… everything I've done so far and the things I've planned."

He lifted his head, staring at me curiously.

"Is it okay? Should I scale back? Because I don't need to do all of this. All I need is you."

He smiled a lopsided, sleepy, yet satisfied smile, and my heart turned over. "What else do you have planned?"

I smiled. "So keep it?"

He nodded once.

I pulled him back against me.

"Ethan?"

"Hm?"

"You know that all I need is you too. Right?"

I kissed the top of his head. "I know, puppy. I know."

That's why I'm going to make sure this is a magical Christmas for you.

4

———

Cold air blew along the streets, whipping around buildings, tugging at the scarves people wore, and making sure everyone knew winter was here.

People still walked the streets because that's what you did in New York City. Especially in the Grimms. I didn't really like the cold. I spent far too long living in it to really enjoy it. But it was different today.

Today, the cold air was less biting as it carried with it the scent of pine and the promise of fresh snow. I was tucked into a warm coat with a scarf and hat. On my feet was a brand-new pair of red boots Ethan gave to me at breakfast along with a pair of Sherpa-lined red mittens.

"I don't want you getting cold today," he said.

So no, the cold seemed a lot less frigid today. Maybe because my heart was so warm.

"The place looks great, Mr. Holly!" I announced,

standing back to take in the tiny makeshift shack that served as the Grimms only tree stand.

"It's a bunch of plywood and nails, Fletcher. It's hardly a castle," Mr. Holly grumbled. "C'mon and hang these wreaths up there."

"Okay!" I said, jumping to work.

Because it was just a temporary stand, it really was basically a box framed out of wood, lined with some unpainted plywood nailed into place. We hung thick sheets of plastic around the openings at the sides and back to help keep out the wind. There was a rectangular window in the front, also lined with plywood, boasting a small counter made of the same.

Inside the little shack was jammed with tree tags, the cashbox, twine, and a bunch of other stuff we might need. There was a small coffeepot too, but honestly, I thought the stuff inside looked like sludge, and I didn't understand how or why Mr. Holly drank it.

The plastic rippled a bit with the wind as I got to work hanging some of the handmade pine wreaths beneath the counter—aka I just nailed them up.

Then I hung some above the window for display. When I was done, I stepped back to admire my handiwork. The little shack was also lined with some colored lights.

On both sides, trees lined the sidewalk, leaning up against wooden stands. They were in various sizes and shapes. Some of them had long pine needles and some had short. We also had this machine that you could feed the trees through, and it would wrap them up in plastic netting to make it easier for people to carry them home.

"Fletcher!" Mr. Holly yelled from across the street.

"Yes?" I waved.

"Come get these!"

Jogging across the street, I looked in the back of an old pickup truck to see stacks of tree stands. "Got a deal on these. Thought we could sell them this year."

"I'll make sure they're right up front!"

He made a sound. "You haven't changed a bit."

I stopped midreach for the first stack. "What do you mean?"

"Means I expected ya to come in here acting like some richie. Didn't expect you to actually work."

I made a face. "I'd never do that. I love this place! Thanks for having me back this year, Mr. H."

A small smile formed on his lips, and he made another gruff sound. "All right then, get to work."

Dragging the first stack of stands out of the truck, I carried them across the street. They were heavy, but I didn't mind the work.

I was dragging the second batch out of the truck when familiar voices came from close by.

"What the hell are you doing?"

I spun as Beau and Daeshim approached. "Hey, guys!" I called. "What are you doing here?"

"We came to get a tree," Beau said.

Daeshim made a face. "Beau came to get a tree. I came to make sure no one was hassling you."

"You don't want a tree?" I asked.

Beau made a noise. "It doesn't matter because our brother is selling them, and we're getting one."

"You have to get a tree, Daeshim! It's Christmas," I told him.

"Christmas is stupid.'"

"Then you should get along with it just fine," Beau snapped.

Beau was the most amicable guy of all of us, but he and Daeshim bickered constantly. They were way worse than Neo and Earth ever were. Sometimes I worried about them being roommates.

"We're almost all set up," I told them, gesturing to the stand. "After I bring all these stands over, I'll help you guys."

"You're hauling all that by yourself?" Beau asked.

"Well, Mr. Holly can't do it." I leaned in to whisper, "He's old."

Daeshim laughed.

"Isn't anyone else working?"

I shook my head. "Not right now. But someone will be here later."

"We'll help you," Daeshim said, grabbing a stack of stands and thrusting them into Beau's middle.

Oomph! All the air rushed out of Beau with the hit.

"Are they too heavy?" he mocked. "Want me to take some of them back?"

"Screw off," Beau muttered, hefting them higher.

I reached for the stack from before.

"Are you wearing mittens?" Daeshim asked, pausing to stare at my outstretched hands.

Feeling a little shy, I pulled my hands against my chest. "Ethan gave them to me so my hands won't get cold."

Daeshim jostled when Beau kicked him. "What the hell was that for?" he growled.

"Like you don't know," Beau muttered. "Leave him alone."

Daeshim turned back to me. "I think they're cute, Fletch."

The three of us carried the rest of the stands across the street, stacking them up.

"Fletcher!" Mr. Holly boomed from inside the shack. "You need to hang these lights!" He came out the small door carrying a bundle of green wire with large, round, clear bulbs on them.

"Look, Mr. H! We have our first customers."

"You bullying this kid?" Daeshim asked, stepping up to Mr. Holly.

"Daeshim!" I gasped. I was so shocked at his accusation I didn't even yell at him for calling me a kid. "Mr. Holly is my boss!"

"Looks to me like he thinks you're his slave."

"Now see here," Mr. Holly said, drawing himself up. "Don't you be coming to my place with that mouth. Fletcher came to work, and that's exactly what he's doing."

Daeshim sniffed. "Why is he the only one working?"

"I'm not!" I insisted. Geez. He was as bad as Earth. Turning to my boss, I said, "I like hanging lights. I'll do it right away."

"Ladder's over there," Mr. Holly grumped.

"I'll help you, Fletch," Beau offered, taking some of the lights and one of the stepladders to move down the line of trees.

Once mine was set up, I put my booted foot on the bottom rung.

"I'll hold it for you. Be careful." Daeshim cautioned.

"Thanks!"

"What about me?" Beau called from down the block.

"What about you?" Daeshim called back.

Beau muttered some things I was probably glad I couldn't hear.

"You shouldn't be so mean to him. Beau is the nicest brother out of all of us," I told him.

"Nice?" He scoffed. "You try living with him."

"I did. For a few years," I pointed out.

He made a rude sound but said nothing else. I hung

the lights, and then we moved to the next strand. Daeshim stood by my ladder then too.

When we were finished, I was so excited I slipped on my way down the ladder.

Gasping, I grappled for the rungs.

Riiip.

Oomph.

Daeshim's steady hands caught me, keeping me from hitting the ground. "See? That old geezer has no business putting you on a ladder."

"Me slipping is not his fault," I argued, straightening away and noticing the rip in my jeans. "Thank you."

"*Ahh!*" Beau called, and we both turned in time to see him and the ladder tip over.

"Beau!" I shouted, rushing past the trees. "Are you okay?"

"I'm never going to hear the end of this," he muttered, straightening the beanie on his head. "I'm fine."

"Are you sure?" I asked, picking up the ladder.

Daeshim strolled up, dark eyes unreadable. "Maybe if you did more than sit behind a computer all day, you wouldn't fall over."

"Fuck off."

"It's Christmas!" I insisted, stepping between them. "And you're brothers."

"We are not!" they both demanded.

"Maybe I should call Earth," I announced, reaching into my coat for my cell. If they were arguing enough to insist they weren't family, he should know.

"No," Beau said, his voice much softer than before. "You're right. It's Christmas. We came to see you and get a tree. So how about you show us the best one you have?"

"We have lots of good ones!" I exclaimed. Then I slid a glance at Daeshim. "You'll get along?"

Daeshim grunted. "Yeah. Let's get a tree."

The sky was a bit gray and the sidewalk felt a bit dark, but when Mr. Holly switched on the lights we'd just hung, a warm glow cast over everything.

Nearby, Mr. Russo pulled up with his roasted chestnut stand and started setting up. I waved at him and Mr. Garcia who was also setting up his hot chocolate stand.

After strolling the long line of trees, I pulled one out, setting it down in the middle of the sidewalk. "How about this one?" I announced. "It would look great in the apartment."

Beau stepped back, taking in its shape and size. "I like it."

"It's ugly," Daeshim announced.

Beau ignored him. "We'll take it."

"Do you need a tree stand?" I asked, hauling it toward the machine to wrap it up.

"Yeah," Beau said.

"You should get a wreath too! Put it on the front door."

"No." Daeshim refused.

"I'll buy it," I said, going around the counter to pick one with a bright-red bow. "Think of it as a thank-you for helping me here today."

"Thanks, bro," Beau said, pulling the tree up once I tied off the netting around it.

The scent of roasting chestnuts wafted over, and I breathed deep. Glancing up at the lights overhead and then at my brother standing on the other side of the counter with a tree and a wreath, I smiled.

"Merry Christmas," I told him.

Beau smiled. "Merry Christmas, Fletch."

I hit a few buttons on the machine and then told them their total.

Beau looked at Daeshim.

"What?"

"Pay him."

Daeshim's lip curled. "You wanted that tree, not me."

It made me wonder something. "Did you celebrate Christmas in Korea?"

Daeshim glanced at me. "Not much." His voice was gruff.

I nodded solemnly. "I never celebrated either until I met our brothers."

His eyes narrowed. "Yeah, right."

Beau hit him in the stomach.

For once, Daeshim looked contrite. "For real?"

I nodded again. "My mom was mean like yours," I whispered. A look moved behind his eyes that I couldn't quite read, but I knew I didn't like it. So I shifted the subject to better things. "Maybe give it a try this year. You might like it better now that you're with us."

The scowl dropped from his face, so I figured that meant he'd try.

Rushing out of the little shack, I threw my arms around him. "Merry Christmas, Daeshim! Thank you for coming to help and get a tree."

He didn't hug me back, but he did pat me on the shoulder, and that was good enough. When I stepped back, he handed me a stack of cash.

"I'll get your change."

"Keep it."

My eyes widened. "What?"

"Keep it. Get yourself some hot chocolate."

I hugged him again.

"I'm the one that fell on my ass helping you hang lights," Beau complained, rubbing his hip.

"Are you hurt?" I worried, turning to face him. Beside me, I felt Daeshim's attention sharpen, but he said nothing at all.

"I'm fine," Beau muttered.

The tree slipped from his grasp when I knocked into him for a hug, but Daeshim caught it before it could hit the sidewalk. "Thanks, Beau!"

"If you have time, come by and help me decorate it," he said, fondness in his voice.

"Daeshim will help you," I offered.

"Hell no, I won't."

"But you said you'd try," I refuted.

He frowned, and I smiled.

"Get some hot chocolate before you go!" I told them, going back into the shack to finish ringing up their tree.

When I came out again, I glanced down the sidewalk to see them standing in front of the hot cocoa cart, arguing.

I felt bad for their tree. It was going to be in some kind of hostile environment.

I worked for a while longer, adding more lights and moving trees as the stand grew busier. Fat, lazy snowflakes started drifting down from the gray sky in the early afternoon, and I sank onto a bench beside some trees. I watched a couple stroll along the sidewalk, hands clasped as they went through the trees, choosing one. I smiled, thinking of Ethan, wondering how his day was going.

"This one!" a small voice insisted from the opposite end of the sidewalk. "I like this one!"

Turning from the smiling couple, I watched a little

boy of no more than six race between two trees with a blue beanie on his head. "Dad! Dad!"

A second later, he reappeared. His face appeared worried. "Dad?"

I jogged over to where the boy was, bending down. "Hi, are you lost?"

He shook his head. "No, but my dad is!"

"Did you come here with him?"

He nodded. "To get a real tree!"

"How about I help you find him?" I offered.

"Okay!" the boy said, pushing his bare hand into my gloved one.

I glanced down at where he held. "Where's your gloves?"

He shrugged. "Don't have any." Then, "Dad!" he hollered.

We started through the trees, down one row and then the other I'd added. Just when I started to worry, I heard a man calling out.

"Chad!"

"Dad, here I am!" The boy waved his arm.

Alarmed, his father jogged over. "Who are you?" he demanded, taking in the way the boy held my hand.

"Fletcher. I work here," I replied.

"He was helping me find you."

The man nodded. "Well, thank you for helping him." Turning to the kid, he said, "Chad, I told you not to wander off."

"But, Dad, I found the perfect tree! Come see!" He let go of my hand to grab his dad's and tugged him back through the trees.

I followed along, listening to the kid chatter. Conflicting emotions of happiness and sadness warred within me. I decided to focus more on the happy feelings than the sad.

"Ta-da!" he said, presenting the tree that was still leaning on its side. "This one!"

"It seems awfully big." The man was skeptical.

"It's not," Chad insisted.

"You can't even see it while it's leaning like that," his dad refuted.

"I can help with that," I announced, moving to pull the tree out and stand it up on the sidewalk.

"It's the best!" the boy declared, bouncing around.

I liked his energy.

The dad, however, didn't seem as excited. "I don't know." He hedged, leaning in to look at the tag hanging from one of the branches. He grimaced slightly upon seeing the price.

"I think it's too big. Why don't we check out some of the smaller ones? Over there—"

"But, Dad, I like this one. This is the best first real tree ever!"

The man cleared his throat.

"It really is the best one." I agreed, earning a hateful glare from the man. Reaching over, I plucked the tag off the tree. "And it's on sale!"

"It is?" The boy jumped up and down.

"Yep, opening day special."

The man stared at me openly, no longer hostile but cautious. "How much is it?"

"Twenty dollars," I announced, tucking the tag into my jeans.

The man's glare reappeared. "What game are you playing?"

"No game," I replied, not ruffled by his ire. I understood it. "Just a special, like I said."

"If there's a sale, where's the sign?"

Turning a little more toward the man and away from his son, I said, "There isn't a sale," I admitted. "But I would like to help a dad give his son a good Christmas."

"I don't need your charity."

Pride was big here in the Grimms, something else I understood. "It's not charity. It's a thank-you for being the kind of parent I wish I had when I was his age."

That struck the man quiet for long moments. Then he tilted his head. "Fletcher, you said?"

I nodded.

"You that guy from around here that was kidnapped from a bunch of richies?"

I nodded again.

The little bit of silence that lapsed between us erupted when Chad burst between us. "Can we get it now?"

The man glanced down at the boy, his face softening. "Yeah, son. You picked a good one."

I smiled.

Once it was wrapped and ready to go, the man handed me his twenty dollars, and I quietly added the rest of the balance due out of my own pocket.

"Decorate it really nice, okay?" I told Chad.

"We will!" he said, already skipping off toward the hot chocolate.

"Hey, ah, thanks," his dad said when the boy was out of earshot.

"Merry Christmas." I smiled, then moved off to help someone else.

"Are you selling these trees or giving them away?" A very familiar, grumpy voice wanted to know.

"Earth!" I exclaimed, spinning around. "You're here!"

He patted my back when I hugged him.

"Did you come to get a tree?" Then I glanced around. "Where's V?"

"She's at her shop. I'll bring her by later, and we'll get a tree then."

"Okay."

"But, ah, maybe you can get me a wreath, and I'll bring it to her. She can make it look girly and hang it on her shop door."

I nodded. "There was one really nice one, and I kept it behind the counter because I knew she'd like it. Mr. Holly yelled at me, but I still hid it back there anyway."

Earth's eyes turned into half-moon shapes. "What do you mean he yelled at you?"

I waved off his ire. "It's fine. I told him I was going to buy it."

He made a rude sound. "Anyone else been hassling you?"

"People are hassling you?" Neo butted right into the conversation, appearing from behind a tree.

"Hey, Neo!" I would have hugged him, but he had a cup of hot chocolate in his hand. "Here," he said, voice a little gruff. "I bought this for you."

"Wow, you did?"

"It's cold. And you probably haven't even stopped bouncing around since you got here."

"Thanks!" I took the cup and lifted it to my lips right away.

"It's hot!" both Neo and Earth exclaimed at the same time.

I rolled my eyes. "I'm not a baby." I reminded them. I don't even know why I bothered. Then I took a big sip. It burned my tongue, but I pretended like it didn't. "It's so good. Thanks for bringing it."

"Now what's this about people giving you a hard time?" he asked as Earth's near-black eyes settled on me.

"Daeshim asked me the same thing," I muttered. *They're just like Ethan.* That made me pause. Lowering the cup from my lips, I asked, "Did Ethan call everyone and tell them to come check on me?"

Neo pretended like he didn't hear.

"My brother was here?" Earth wanted to know.

Ethan totally called them all.

I nodded. "He and Beau came to get a tree. They fought the whole time. I almost called you."

Earth frowned. "Why?"

"So you could make them stop," I said. Wasn't it obvious? "Maybe they shouldn't live together. They fight worse than you and Neo."

Neo laughed.

"They're fine," Earth grumped.

"Where's Ivory?"

"Work. You'll see her later."

"I will?" I wondered.

"Fletcher!"

My brothers turned at the sound of Mr. Holly's bellow.

Suddenly, Mr. H looked like he'd swallowed a lemon. "Oh, Earth. Neo. I didn't know you were here."

"Obviously," Earth intoned.

"You come to get a tree?"

"Fletcher put a wreath aside for Virginia," he replied.

"Oh, that was for her?"

"Excuse me," someone on the other side of the stand called. Mr. Holly used the distraction to flee.

"You scare everyone." I accused Earth.

"Good," he deadpanned.

"Pick me out a tree," Neo gestured to the trees nearby.

"You and Ivory already have a tree. More than one." I reminded him.

"They're fake. We need a real one."

I nodded. "We still have to get a real one too."

"Come on, then. I don't have all day," Earth complained.

"You should get a tree for the bar," I told him.

"No."

I made a sound. "People would like it."

I could feel him glowering at me as I looked around for the perfect tree for Neo. "Who cares?"

"Such a scrooge," I declared, then pulled out a tree to hold out for Neo. "How about this one?" I asked him.

Before he could answer, Earth crossed his arms over his chest. "Fine. Maybe a small one."

I spun from Neo. "Really?"

"You have to decorate it."

"Okay! We can put a Santa hat on the top." I planned.

Earth groaned, and Neo snickered. "Sucker."

Earth gave him the finger. "Fuck you."

After they each bought a tree and the wreath, they left, and Mr. Holly came behind the counter. His voice was gruff, his body language slightly awkward.

"You've sold a lot of trees already today." He scratched beneath his hat. "Keep up the good work."

The compliment meant a lot coming from bad-tempered old Mr. Holly, and my heart expanded. "Thank you!" I said, hugging him.

"All right now, that's enough. Get back to work, or you're fired."

Smiling, I went back to work.

5

ETHAN

I STOOD BACK AND WATCHED FOR A WHILE. HE WAS THE kind of man who didn't abandon kindness, even when it was a heavy gift to bear.

I'd known men who suffered far less in their lives who couldn't even afford half the kindness Fletcher gave eagerly on a daily basis.

Yet people called him the poor one.

How glaringly untrue.

He seemed in his element, moving from one place to the next, checking tree after tree. Even from a distance, I could see the pink on his cheeks and the tip of his nose from being in the winter wind all day. Funny how those charming spots of color existed because of the cold, but seeing him wear them made my heart warm.

Occasionally, the wind would carry his laughter to me, and my stomach would tighten a bit because the sound was so pure. Smiling to myself, I watched him hang a pine wreath below the hideous counter window. If you could call it that. The tree stand he dearly loved was frankly a downgrade from a shack… yet oddly, I saw its charm.

Colored lights lit up the odd shape of the place, sheets of plastic blew around, and somewhere nearby, a child was having a tantrum.

But the scent of chestnuts mingled with the winter air, underscored with a note of chocolate. White lights bobbed overhead, swaying with the breeze. A few benches down, a man was busking on the sidewalk, playing some jazzy Christmas tune on a saxophone.

As I stood there and watched the man I loved and snow fell lazily from the sky, I understood. I saw with perfect clarity how he found Christmas here and why it meant so much to him.

If my eyes started to water, it was only because the wind was so bitter.

Finished with the wreath, Fletch spun, the ends of his scarf trailing out behind him as he disappeared between some trees and came back just moments later holding the hand of a red-faced child. Clearly, this was the one throwing the tantrum, but now she was holding Fletcher's hand, and he was pointing up at the lights.

Swallowing turned impossible, and a new feeling wrapped around my soul. Fact: we often referred to Fletch as a baby, and in truth, his innocence could sometimes be childlike. But Fletcher was all man. Wise beyond his years with experiences I wished he didn't have. People often didn't believe or comprehend the vileness he lived. They couldn't. His kind heart and innocence shielded it too well.

But I knew.

I knew the reason he still had all the wonder of a

young heart in the body of a man. He'd been so buried in hate it practically repressed him.

As I watched him beneath the warm glow of cheap lights, holding the hand of a child who looked up at him like he hung the moon, I thought what a wonderful dad he would make. Capable of joy and love but also of strength and resilience.

Using the tail end of my Burberry scarf, I patted the wind out of my eyes. When they cleared, I saw Fletcher holding a tree out from the rest, showing it to the girl and likely her mother.

The little girl was clapping, the mother looking a little less excited.

Slyly, Fletcher snagged the tag off a nearby branch and slipped it into his pocket. When he withdrew his hand, there was a candy cane sticking out of his mitten.

The child's squeal carried to my ears, and Fletch surrendered the candy. Then, angling toward the mother a bit more, he said something I couldn't hear and then smiled.

In a burst of movement, the woman rushed forward, knocking into Fletch, making the branches on the tree he still held shake.

I stiffened, stepping into the street, but then my feet stalled.

She was hugging him. He gave her a couple pats on her back, and then she drew away.

I watched him expertly run the tree through the netting machine—and if I noticed he looked sexy doing that physical activity, well, that's my business. Then he set it on a wagon of sorts and then lifted the girl to sit beside it.

He waved good-bye to the woman as she tugged

along the wagon with the tree and her daughter. No money changed hands.

When she was gone, he went behind the counter.

Oh, my heart. My heart might beat right out of my chest.

An obnoxious honking sound broke into the moment. I mean, I knew this was the city, but good heavens, the audacity!

Hoooonk. Honk!

Straightening, I spun, glaring in the direction the horrid sound came from. Recoiling almost instantly, I raised an arm to shield my eyes from the harsh headlights.

"Hey, bozo! Get out of the street!" hollered the driver of the car blinding me, leaning out the window like some dog.

How uncouth.

Hoonk!

I'd forgotten I stepped into the street while watching Fletch. The man honked again.

"It'd be quieter if he just hit me," I muttered, quickly moving back to the sidewalk.

His engine revved, and he shot by.

By the sound of his engine, he would likely break down on the next block over.

Forgetting him, I turned back to Fletch. It only took half a second to find him, but when I did, it was to see someone angrily jab a finger into his chest and exclaim something I couldn't hear.

The instinct to protect propelled me forward, anger slashing through me like a hot lightning rod. If someone wanted to hassle Fletcher, well, they could go through me to do it.

This time I paid no mind to the honking horns or the

god-awful screeching of brakes as I strode across the street without pause. The flaps of my long red wool coat floated around my legs, the plaid Burberry scarf plastered against my chest.

"It's a clear violation!" a man insisted.

"It's Christmas!" Fletcher exclaimed.

"The law is the law," he intoned.

My back teeth snapped together. I knew that voice.

My boots stomped over the sidewalk as I hurried over, both men too involved in their spat to notice me coming.

"C'mon, Fig, can't you just give us a break?"

"You think 'cause you got some fancy last name now—"

"My last name is still the same," Fletcher insisted, but Officer Fig just steamrolled right over his words.

"You can't just set up trees all willy-nilly all over the sidewalk. Here in the Grimms, we got rules, and our rules can't be bought. Now clear it out, Fletch, or I'll be forced to haul you in."

He crossed his arms over his chest, chin jutting out. "You can't arrest me!"

"Watch me." Fig threatened.

"What did I tell you about the odd vendetta you have against Fletcher?" I cut into their conversation, owning it with my even-toned voice.

Fletcher rotated, his eyes lighting up and a grin breaking over his features. "You came!"

I was so used to him plowing into me for hugs that I didn't even wobble when he did it this time, wrapping his arms around my waist, pressing his hands against my back.

"Did you think I wouldn't?" I asked, forgetting I was angry.

"I just figured I'd meet you at home."

I made a noise. "Well, I decided to bring home to you."

His arms tightened around my waist for a fraction of a second before pulling back and gesturing to the stand. "Isn't it awesome?"

"I admit it's very charming."

Fletcher beamed and started to speak, only to be so rudely interrupted.

"Charming like a bad case of monkey butt," Fig announced. "And it's also unlawful. Take it down."

"How exactly is this stand unlawful?" I inquired.

Fig drew up, puffing out his chest beneath the unfortunate brown jacket he wore. "It's crowding the streets, creating a fire hazard, and breaking all kinds of codes!"

"I'm not taking it down. You can't make me!" Fletcher snapped, but then I felt his hand at the back of my coat.

He always did that for security. For comfort. Which he clearly needed because Fig was threatening him.

A pair of silver handcuffs jangled loudly when he pulled them from his belt.

I laughed. It wasn't jolly.

Several sets of eyes shifted to me. The sudden shift in the air made Fletcher's hand tighten.

"What did I tell you about constantly trying to arrest Fletcher?"

Fig's eyes narrowed. "I gave him a police order. He's belligerent and noncompliant."

"Just because you can use those words in a sentence doesn't mean they apply to the situation," I spat. Taking an ominous step toward the officer, I let my upper lip curl. "I saw you put your hands on him."

Fig's eyes widened. "W-what? No."

"I stood right over there and watched you shove your finger into his chest."

"E—" Fletcher tried. I slid a glance at him, and he stopped speaking.

"If you so much as breathe in his direction ever again, I'll have your job." This threat was getting old. Perhaps I should just do it already. Empty threats were of no use to me.

"You can't do that!"

I laughed again. "I'll buy that whole building you call a station and then toss you out on your bigoted ass."

He sputtered. "I am not bigoted!" He swallowed. "Threatening an officer is a crime."

I raised an eyebrow. "And what is harassing civilians?"

"Fletcher!" a new voice snapped. I liked it about as much as I liked Fig.

Fletcher's hand dropped from my coat. "Here, Mr. Holly!"

"What the hell are you doing out here? This ain't social hour. You're supposed to be working."

I turned, making the man stop midstride. "And who are you?" I asked coolly.

"Mr. Holly of Holly Trees. I own this place."

"Did I just hear you bullying Fletcher?"

Fletch groaned.

"What the hell is it with you people? Coming by here all day, asking me the same damn thing. He's my employee! It's my job to tell him what to do."

"Well, with ethics like that, no wonder the walls of your establishment are plastic," I deadpanned.

"Now see here—"

"Wait!" Fletcher announced, inserting himself in the middle of everything. "Mr. Holly, don't be mad. Ethan is just upset because when he got here, Fig was yelling at me." Fletcher turned his round eyes up to mine. "Ethan, this stand is temporary. Of course the walls are just made crudely. It would hardly make sense to pour profit into something he would just take down."

I smiled. "Spoken like a true businessman." Leaning in toward his ear, I said, "You're starting to use big words like me."

His already pink cheeks turned deeper. The urge to kiss him silly came over me.

"Wait just one minute." Fig interrupted. "Whose place is this?"

"Like you don't know," Mr. Holly retorted. "I've been running this place since you were barely outta diapers." Then crossing his arms over his chest, he tacked on, "And in all that time, you never bought a tree from me."

"Why would I waste my money on a dead tree?" Fig sniped back.

Fletcher gasped.

This was ridiculous.

"I didn't know you were here, Mr. Holly. I thought this richie here bought you out and took over."

"I told you I couldn't shut it down," Fletcher said. "I don't run the place."

"I ain't no sellout," Mr. Holly boomed. "This is my place and always will be. Now if you ain't here for a tree, get out. You're taking up space for paying customers."

I glanced at Fletch, quietly lifting a brow. Fletcher giggled.

"The worst time of the year," Fig muttered, turning to go.

I caught him by the back of the coat. "Excuse me."

Fig glared over his shoulder.

"Are you seriously just leaving and forgetting about

all the *violations* this place is breaking because you found out it's not Fletcher's?"

Fig snorted, pulling free from my grasp. "First, you were mad I was gonna arrest him, and now you aren't because I'm not?"

Cocking my head to the side, I glared at the officer. "What do you have against Fletcher?"

"Ethan," Fletcher called, stepping closer to my side. "It's fine. Just let him go."

"How many more times should I overlook this mistreatment?" I asked, not glancing away from Fig.

A mitten-covered hand curled around mine. "It's Christmas. I want to show you the trees."

Finally pulling my gaze from Fig, I glanced at my lover. Those honey-colored orbs could distract me from anything.

Turning my back on the officer, I tightened my hand around Fletcher's. "Okay, give me the tour."

Fig made a strangled noise, and I whipped my head around, glaring over my shoulder. He swallowed thickly and started away.

"Get some hot chocolate, Fig!" Fletch called out. "It will make you less of a grinch!"

"Bah, humbug!" he yelled.

"Get back to work!" Mr. Holly snapped.

"I sincerely hope you haven't been speaking to him like this all day." I kept my tone level.

Clearing his throat, he said, "He knows I don't mean nothing by it. He's a good kid."

"I'm not a kid," Fletcher insisted.

"To me, when you're younger than forty, you're a kid!"

We held hands, walking under the lights bobbing in the wind overhead. They cast a glow onto the sidewalk and on the trees. A fine dusting of snow coated the pine branches, nearby benches, and edges of the sidewalk.

"We've been so busy today." Fletcher rambled on about everything, pulling out trees to show them to me before putting them back and moving to another one that looked exactly the same.

"Puppy," I called, and he let go of the tenth tree he was about to pick up. When his eyes met mine, they were soft. "Come here."

He came immediately, eyes never leaving me. Our chests nearly bumped, he stopped so close.

Moving the slight distance between us, I closed it, bringing our bodies flush. "Were you warm enough today?"

Emotion swam in his glimmering stare. Full lips I loved to kiss turned up just enough to tell me he was pleased. "Yes. So many times I saw people who needed gloves, and I thought to give them mine, but I couldn't."

I made a soft noise, encouraging him to continue.

"I couldn't give these away because you gave them to me this morning. Because you didn't want me to be cold."

"And are you cold?" I murmured, caressing his face with my gaze. My heart beat slow and unevenly because I yearned to pull him in but couldn't.

He shook his head. "No."

"Why do you have so many holes in your jeans?" I asked.

Startled, he glanced down at his lower half as if he didn't realize they were ripped in several places. Sheepish, he shrugged. "Tree stands are a lot of work."

"Mm. And you're sure you aren't cold?"

"Kiss me."

I kissed him right there on the street under a dark

winter sky surrounded by strangers and trees. He tasted faintly of chocolate, so I went back for another taste.

"Came to buy a tree and am getting a show for free."

I didn't jolt away. Even when Fletcher stiffened, I pulled him in and finished the kiss before easing back and glancing over my shoulder.

"Ander. How nice to see you." Turning my eyes to the woman at his side, I smiled. "Emogen, you look beautiful, as always."

She smiled. "How ya doing, Ethan?"

"Hi, guys!" Fletcher skirted around me to hug them both. "Did you come for a tree?"

"Of course," Emogen said.

"We would have been here sooner, but we wanted to wait for it to get dark. Enjoy the lights," Ander told us.

"Beau helped me hang them," Fletcher said, not even blinking at the explanation.

We all knew that Ander probably felt more comfortable with the sun down. Less staring that way. Easier to hide inside the hoodie pulled over his head.

"Em made me hang a thousand lights at our place too," Ander bemoaned.

Emogen rolled her eyes. "A little labor is good for you."

"I can't wait to see them," Fletcher said, then, "What kind of tree do you want?"

"The biggest one you have!" Ander replied.

Fletcher led us to the spot where the bigger trees were, reaching out to grab one. My chest came up against his back when I leaned in to reach around him. "I'll get it," I whispered.

Not moving out of our shared space, Fletcher made a face. "I've been getting them all day."

I kissed his wrinkled-up nose. "Well, you don't have to now because I'm here."

"You're my favorite," he confided.

My heart tumbled into my stomach. "Mine too," I echoed.

Pulling away, he gestured for me to tug up the tree. I held it out while Ander and Emogen looked it over and then held out a few more for good measure.

In the end, they settled on the first one Fletcher suggested, and they purchased it along with a tree stand and a wreath.

"Thanks, guys!" Fletcher said.

"It will be decorated when you come to the house for the party," Emogen told him.

Ander made a rude sound. "I'm not stringing any more lights, Em."

"Then I'm not making any more Christmas cookies," she countered.

He made a face, and I chuckled. "Have fun with that."

Ander scoffed. "You hired it out, didn't you? She wouldn't let me."

"Ethan strung them around our Marvel tree," Fletcher put in.

"A Marvel tree?" Em asked, interested.

Fletcher nodded. "Come see it, okay?"

"Wouldn't miss it." Emogen agreed.

"We still have one tree left to get, for our living room. We'll string lights on that too. Right, E?"

"Whatever you want," I told him.

Emogen's eyes widened in surprise. "You mean you've been here working, and you haven't gotten a tree yet?"

"I've been so busy helping other people, I forgot!"

Fletcher said, brow furrowing. "We can pick one out right now."

"Uhh," I said, glancing around at the trees that honestly were about half the size of the one I had scheduled for delivery tomorrow.

Ander gave me a knowing look, and I hid my grimace.

"Ethan?" Fletcher asked, hand laying on my arm.

I smiled. "Let's pick one out now. Of course, we have to get one from the best stand in New York."

Emogen and Fletcher moved off to look at one Fletcher pointed to, and Ander moved up to my side. "Guess we're both getting a crash course in how those that aren't from the Upper East Side do Christmas."

I laughed under my breath. "Yes. I suppose so."

"It's way better." Ander's voice was soft as he gazed after Emogen.

"Way, way better." I agreed.

When they were gone, Fletcher gasped. "I know the perfect tree!"

And he thinks I'm dramatic.

"Well, let's see it," I said, gesturing for him to lead the way.

Instead of rushing off into a row of trees, he ran around the plastic-wrapped shack, disappearing into the darkness behind it.

"Fletcher!" I called after him.

His head appeared around the corner. "Just wait right there."

I waited, but it was a test of patience because all I could think about was what could be lurking behind such a crudely made ramshackle building that was plucked in the middle of the ghetto.

A heavy thump and what sounded like cans scattering around were followed by a low swear.

"Fletcher!" I yelled, starting toward the back.

But then he appeared, stepping through the plastic. The only thing visible behind a wild bunch of pine branches were his ripped jeans, red boots, and one mitten-covered hand.

"Here it is!" he declared, carrying it to the sidewalk to plunk it down. A few needles fell off the branches, littering the sidewalk beneath it.

"What is that?" I asked dubiously.

"Our perfect tree!"

Oh, he couldn't be serious. I squinted, tilting my head. "Is it heavy?" I worried, preparing to step forward. "Straighten your arm."

"It's not heavy. It just grew a little crooked."

Oh. He was serious.

"I know it's a little sparse." He started.

"There's a hole in one side," I pointed out. I moved closer. "And is that a bird's nest?"

Fletcher glanced at where I stared. It was indeed a bird's nest. "See, it's so great, even a bird made it a home," he said.

"It's not very tall. We have high ceilings," I observed.

The tree was about his height, which meant it wasn't even six feet.

"We already have a bunch of tall trees."

The top branch where one usually put a star or some grand ornament was thin and already bending under its own weight.

To speak frankly, it was probably the ugliest tree I'd ever seen.

"Don't you want to get one of the fuller ones over there?" I wondered.

Fletcher's face fell a bit. "But, E, if we don't get this one, Mr. Holly will throw it out in tomorrow's trash. When I first unloaded it, he told me to strip its branches to make a few wreaths we could sell. He told me this was too ugly and no one would want to buy it."

Fletcher looked back at the sad little tree.

"I couldn't do it, so I hid it behind the shack. But then I remembered we need a tree! It might be a little crooked and might need some extra ornaments, but it's still a good tree. Just because it's not perfect like the others..." He paused. "It's a misfit. Just like me. You love me the way I am, right?"

Everyone. Meet our new tree.

"Oh, yes, puppy. I love you exactly as you are, and if this tree is anything like you, then I love it too."

He smiled.

It took me a minute to swallow past the lump in my throat, but when I did, I motioned for him to hold it out again. "Hold it up. Let me look at it."

Fletcher did, and I walked around it, carefully looking it over. When I was done, I stopped right beside him. "You're right. It is our most perfect tree."

He turned suspicious. "Are you just saying that?"

"I don't just say things, puppy. Let's wrap it up and take it home, okay?"

He fell into my chest, and since he was still holding the tree, I ended up holding both of them. Even though it was poking me in the eye and nose, my chest felt tight.

"Merry Christmas, Fletcher," I whispered, holding him a little tighter.

"Merry Christmas, Ethan. I love you."

"Come on, then," I said, taking the tree from his grasp. Let's figure out how to stuff this thing into the

Mercedes and get it home. We have plans later that we can't be late for."

"Plans! What plans?"

Leaning in, I pressed a soft kiss to his cold lips. "It's a surprise."

"Come on, then. We have to go!"

He went off to pay for the tree, and I gazed down at the pitiful thing and smiled.

It really was a perfect tree.

6

CHRISTMAS TUNES FLOWED FROM THE SPEAKERS overhead, filling the shop with a merry feeling. The big front window was decorated with flocked pine trees, poinsettias, and baskets of greenery sprinkled with glitter, ornaments, and snowflakes. There was even an old train set chugging around the trees.

Paper snowflakes and white icicle lights hung from the top, and Neo had painted the window itself with snowdrifts at the bottom and snowflakes to make it look like it was snowing inside.

Jingle bells hung over the shop door so every time it opened or closed, it sounded like Santa was coming.

The wooden tables inside Tangled Stems were all decorated with pine swag, ornaments, glitter, and, of course, flower arrangements styled by me.

I even made a wreath out of ribbon and greenery,

which I braided together and then added some holly berry and snow.

My flower shop was small, but it was one of my most favorite places, second only to the new home Earth and I shared upstairs. Having this place was a dream come true, even if it had scared me a little at first.

I mean, I guess all the best dreams are a little frightening, right?

But the people here in the Grimms embraced my little flower shop, and they were all so kind to me. At first, I thought it was because they were all terrified of Earth. Which they were.

But it was easy to tell the ones who were nice out of fear and the ones who genuinely meant it. Most people genuinely meant it. I even had some regular customers who came by every week.

"Won't you guide my sleigh tonight?" I burst out, singing with the music.

A loud snort burst up from the floor, and I nearly dropped the glittered pinecone I was holding. Giggling, I noted the startled look on a sleepy Snort's face as he stared around like he was confused.

"Sing it with me, boy!" I told him, belting out another line.

He made a snorting sound and lifted his nose to smell toward what I was holding. I held it out, and he sneezed.

"Eww!" I squealed, pulling the pinecone back. Glitter sprinkled onto the dog's head. "Well, I don't think it would be appropriate to use this in Mrs. Jameson's arrangement now," I remarked, setting aside the slobbery decoration.

Zilla poked her head out of the hair falling over my shoulder, and Snort heaved a sigh, siding back onto the floor to go back to sleep.

I put a few last-minute and sneeze-free decorations into the small arrangement I was making and then sat back to admire it.

"She's going to love it!" I declared, taking in the small red sleigh bursting with fresh pine, red berries, gold glitter pinecones, and a few red roses.

Setting it in my lap, I wheeled it over to the large cooler against the wall and carefully placed it inside.

The bells on the door jingled, and I smiled. Snort perked up again, glancing in the direction of the door. Butterflies fluttered wildly about beneath my ribs at the chance of seeing Earth.

Ding-ding-ding-ding! Noise erupted from the small bell on the counter with the register, and I knew immediately it was not Earth.

"Coming!" I called out, wheeling back to the counter. "How can I help you today?" I asked, wheeling up to the counter where I'd been working.

"Don't you know how rude it is not to have someone behind the register?" an impatient voice snapped. "Do you make all your customers wait like this?"

I faltered for a second and then smiled. I wasn't exactly a stranger to grumpy people. I lived in the Grimms... and with Earth, who was the grumpiest of them all.

"I'm so sorry, sir," I said, moving a little farther toward the register. "I was putting away an arrangement in the back. Usually, I'm up here. Woul—"

"Well, maybe you should hire more help," he grumbled. His hair was wind-blown, the tips of his ears red from the cold. He held a few bags in his hands, one of them from the bakery on the next block over and one from the store at the end of our street.

"You must be running errands. It's a busy time of

year. Would you like some warm cocoa or coffee? There's a hot drink cart right over there." I gestured across the space to where the small bar sat.

"What I want is to pick up what I ordered."

"Oh! You have a pickup?" I wheeled the rest of the way behind the counter. I felt his stare, the way it lingered on my legs.

I was used to people staring and to their curiosity about me being in a wheelchair. It normally didn't bother me. But right now, it kind of did.

Smiling, I pulled up the order screen. "What is your last name?"

"Brock."

The screen blurred a little when he said that. The smile I was wearing faltered a little but recovered. "Oh, yes. I remember. Your arrangement is in the back. I'll be right back."

He grumbled something I couldn't hear, but I didn't ask him to repeat himself. It probably wasn't very nice.

Customer service was sometimes a challenge. Especially around this time of year. People seemed more harried and short-tempered. But I reminded myself that for so many years, I dreamed of being out around people, of having something of my own. Having an entire shop and home to decorate instead of just one room with no window was so wonderful that a few people with bad attitudes couldn't ruin it.

I told myself that perhaps they just needed someone to be kind to them.

As I pulled the arrangement out of the cooler, my teeth sank into my lip. A little bit of water dripped from my hand down my wrist, slipping under the sleeve of the Christmas sweater I wore.

Bringing it back to the register, I placed it on the counter. "Here it is!" I smiled. "I think it turned out—"

"What in the hell is that?" he roared, jabbing a finger at the small red tin. It was filled with glory-of-the-snow, six red tulips, and two white hyacinths. I added a sparkling white bow around the tin to give it something extra.

"That's your arrangement," I said, knowing things were about to go downhill fast.

"The hell it is!" He gave it a derisive look. How anyone could be so rude to flowers, I would never know. "That is not what I ordered."

"I realize the arrangement you originally ordered included six dramatic red and white superstar amaryllis, but as I explained on the phone this morning when I called you, those flowers were damaged in delivery, and I couldn't use them. Because I had them trucked in, I don't have any others to replace them with."

"Why didn't you order backups?"

"I did. They were damaged too. The truck got into an accident—"

"How is any of this my fault? I'm the paying customer. You take my money, and then you hand me this?" He gestured to the arrangement, and my heart sank.

"Those flowers are beautiful, and you shouldn't tell them otherwise," I said.

He drew back as though I'd shocked him. His laugh rang up to the paper snowflakes hanging from the ceiling.

"Also..." I bravely forged on. "As I said on the phone, I am not charging you for the arrangement because it isn't to your satisfaction. You told me that the arrangement without the superstar would be fine."

CAMBRIA HEBERT

"Well, I changed my mind!"

"You can just leave it here, then." I decided. Those poor tulips were already wilting against his foul demeanor.

His eyes widened so much I saw the whites all around the blue orbs. "Excuse me?"

"I'm very sorry the order was not to your satisfaction. I have some extra roses in the back if—"

He slapped his hand down on the counter with a *bang!* The loud sound made Snort jolt up and come racing around the counter with a growl.

"Ahh!" the man screamed. "What is that?"

"A dog," I deadpanned.

"Of course it is, you twit!" He sneered. "I meant that." He pointed toward me, and I bristled. Then I realized that Zilla had poked her head out of my hair again.

Before I could say anything at all, Earth materialized from somewhere in the shop, slamming a heavy hand down on the ranting man's shoulder.

He opened his mouth to yell, but Earth squeezed, and the man cringed, bending a bit at the knees.

"Help!" he called to me, eyes still bugging from his head. He was going to have a headache later. "I'm being attacked! Don't just sit there! Do something!"

"I'm afraid my legs don't work as well as your mouth," I replied sweetly.

Okay, that wasn't kind. But I couldn't help it.

Rage lit his eyes, and he readied to yell more insults my way.

"Did you just call my woman a twit?" Earth's voice was deadly calm.

Whatever Mr. Brock was about to yell shriveled right there on his tongue. "Did you yell at her and hit something?"

The man whimpered, his knees buckling.

"Earth." I admonished.

He flicked a short, assessing glance at me. "You okay, sprite?"

"Of course!"

He grunted, a sour look on his face, but he let go of the man.

Panting, the angry customer rose to his feet. "How dare you?"

"You new around here?" Earth asked. I didn't like the calm in his tone. It never led to good things.

"I heard about this place from a friend. Said some of the big shots in the Upper East Side get their flowers here," he replied, straightening his coat. "That must have been a lie. She can't even make one simple arrangement, and then she tries to pass off that ugly thing just to get paid!"

Crack!

That was the sound of the man's nose when Earth's fist plowed into it.

Snort barked, I winced, and the man stumbled back, straight for a lovely display of poinsettias. Shooting his hand out, Earth grabbed the man by the coat and yanked him forward, stopping him from crashing into my display.

Then he punched him again.

The whine the man made as he bent at the waist made me feel bad for him.

"Here in the Grimms, we all live by a certain set of rules. A code. And one of those hard rules is that you respect this place. You respect that woman, and you sure as shit don't come around here and insult her. You owe her an apology. Better make it good."

"Earth," I admonished. "Just let him go. He didn't like the flowers."

"Well, I don't like him."

I gave a long, insufferable sigh. It was very hard to reason with him when he got like this.

Too bad the man with the broken nose didn't seem to get the memo. "I'm not apologizing! I'm the customer, and I'm gonna tell everyone what a shit place this is and what a shit—"

Grabbing him by the back of his neck, Earth hauled him up and started walking to the door, dragging the man along with him. He managed to do it with one hand as he reached beneath his leather jacket to pull out his blade.

"Wh-what is that?" the man squealed.

"It's your first-class ticket straight to hell."

The man started fighting, slapping at Earth's arm to get him to release his neck. Earth gave him a bored look and kept dragging.

"Earth, stop it," I called.

"Please! No!" Brock begged. "I'll call the cops."

Earth laughed. "Even the police don't mess with my girl around here."

"Earth!" I bellowed.

He ignored me again.

The man started crying. Reaching out, I grabbed the first thing my hand closed around, a red shatterproof ornament.

I chucked it at Earth. The glittery ball hit him between the shoulders and bounced off, hitting the floor. Then I grabbed the sneezed-on glittered pinecone and threw that at him too. It hit him in the back of the head.

His feet stalled. He glanced over his shoulder, lifting a brow at me. "Did you just throw an ornament at me?"

I lifted my chin. "A slobbery pinecone too."

His eyes narrowed. Everyone was so afraid of that look, but I wasn't. "It's Christmastime," was all I said.

His lip curled, and a whole moody look rolled over his features like a storm cloud. The man sprawled on the floor when Earth let go.

"Get the fuck out of here and don't come back. If I ever see you on my street again, you're dead."

The man scrambled out, the bells slapping against the wooden frame in his haste. When he was gone, Earth slammed the door, threw the lock, and turned the open sign to closed.

"I'm not closed!" I disputed.

"You are now."

"Don't you tell me what to do!"

"Don't push me, sprite." His voice was mild as he approached and sheathed his blade.

Hands sliding beneath my arms, he lifted me out of the wheelchair like I weighed nothing, holding me up so my paralyzed legs and feet dangled over the floor. His arms didn't even tremble with the effort, and I knew it was because he'd been lifting weights.

"He touch you?" he asked, eyes all squinty.

"I'd have brained him!"

His lips twitched. "You okay?"

I rolled my eyes. "He's hardly the first person to ever say mean things to me."

He jolted. "Who else was mean to you?"

I patted his shoulder. "No one."

"I should have killed him."

"You can't kill people at Christmas."

"So I can kill him after New Year's?" I could see him already plotting in that villainous head of his.

"No. You promised."

His whole face softened. "I know, sprite. Why do you think I went so easy on him?"

"You broke his nose," I pointed out.

"'Tis the season."

I giggled. I couldn't help it. Earth's black eyes softened. Actually, everything about him did.

Zilla poked her head out of my hair again.

"Hey, Zil." Earth greeted her.

"She scared that man," I told him, laughing.

"Pansy."

I laughed again, but it turned into a muffled squeak when his lips latched onto mine. His kiss was as it always was: possessive and demanding. I loved that he wasn't all that gentle, not treating me like I was too fragile. But even in his ferocity, I could feel his love. My body relaxed into his attention and the way his mouth worked mine. Sometimes I still marveled at how well my body responded to his, almost as if he'd somehow conditioned me to respond with a few expert strokes of his tongue.

"What are you doing here?" I asked when he finally lifted his head.

"Can't a man come kiss his girl?"

"Anytime you want." I echoed, leaning in to press against his shoulder. My eyes fluttered closed when he stroked my hair.

"I brought you a wreath from the tree stand." His voice was gruff, but he spoke softly. "For the front door."

"Oh, did you already hang it up?" I asked, gazing across the shop.

"So I could just take it back down for you to dump glitter all over it?"

I gasped. "As if I *dump* glitter on everything."

"You have it in your hair."

I smirked. "Well, you have it on the back of your leather jacket."

He glowered.

I patted his shoulder. "Can I see the wreath?"

Sitting me back in my wheelchair, he backtracked across the room to retrieve the wreath, which was full and plain but had a big red bow. "Fletcher picked it for you."

"It's beautiful! I love it! And you're right. It needs glitter."

"Glitter is stupid."

"But I like it," I refuted.

Looking completely annoyed, he reached into the inside of his leather jacket and pulled out a container of silver glitter, thrusting it toward me. "Here."

My heart fluttered, and not even his grumpy, annoyed reaction could erase the sweetness of the gesture. "Earth!" I exclaimed, setting aside the wreath to grab the glitter and hug it into my chest. "You got me glitter?"

He grunted. "Figured if I didn't, you'd just send me back out for it."

I held my arms out, wiggling my fingers at him. The hard angles of his face softened, and he dropped down in front of the chair. Throwing my arms around his neck, I pulled myself close, breathing in his leather and stale cigarette smoke scent. Smiling against his neck, I whispered, "Thank you, Earth. I love it."

"I stole it," he announced. "Couldn't be seen buying that shit." Then to himself, he muttered, "I'd never hear the end of it."

I swallowed down a giggle. He was completely ridiculous. When I pulled back, I kissed his cheek. "Help me decorate the wreath."

"No."

"You're stupid."

He barked a laugh and stood.

"Earth?"

The hesitation in my voice made him squat back down to my level. Reaching out, he tugged on the end of my hair. "What, sweetheart?"

"Aren't you going to ask me?"

His brows furrowed. "Ask you what?"

"What I did to make that man so mad."

His palm curled around my upper arm, his other curling around my hand. He always did that. He always held where I would be able to feel his touch. "You didn't do anything."

I felt my chin jut out. "Maybe I did."

His dark brow arched into his forehead. "Did you run over his foot?"

I gasped. "I'm about to run over yours!"

He laughed. Fingers tightening around my arm, he leaned in, turning sincere. "Whatever you did, I don't care. No one is ever gonna talk to you like that while I'm around."

I whispered, "I love you."

"I love you too, sprite."

"You really won't help me decorate the wreath?"

"We can't. We have somewhere to be," he said, standing once more.

"We do?" Then I remembered. "Oh! We have to get our tree! Fletcher is probably waiting."

He shook his head. "We'll get the tree tomorrow. Fletcher will be there then too."

"But what about today?"

"Today we have other plans."

I searched my mind for anything I could have forgotten, but there was nothing. "What plans?"

"It's a surprise."

The steady rhythm of my heart picked up. "What kind of surprise?"

He mumbled something.

I leaned forward. "What?"

I strained to hear as he mumbled it again, but the moment I understood, I smiled widely as excitement unfurled within in me.

A Christmas surprise.

7

EARTH

I DON'T DO CHRISTMAS.

Well, until Fletcher moved in and always had this sort of longing in his face when he saw Christmas commercials on TV and passed by any shop with a decoration.

I couldn't just let the kid look like that. It gave me indigestion. So I made pancakes on Christmas morning. And dragged home a tree. And maybe we all exchanged presents. They were small, but it made him happy.

This year, we were all a little more spread out than usual. This year, Fletch had Ethan to fawn all over him and make their fancy apartment look like Christmas puked all over it. Good. I wouldn't miss making pancakes for him on Christmas morning.

But I had Virginia this year, and she loved Christmas probably more than Fletcher. So yeah, I'd probably be making pancakes. This year and for every year after. And doing all kinds of shit I didn't want to.

Prime example? Exactly what we were doing tonight.

"But if you won't tell me where we're going, how will I know what to wear?" Virginia asked as the elevator opened up into our newly finished apartment.

It was too white. Too bright, too clean, and there were candles and flowers everywhere.

It was ridiculous and ugly.

She sighed dreamily, rolling out of the box. "I don't think I'll ever get tired of coming home. This place is so beautiful. More than I ever dreamed. But my favorite thing about it is that you're here," Virginia said, glancing over her shoulder as she went ahead into the open space.

Okay, fine. I liked our place. A lot. Even if the windows facing the street were big and let in a lot of light. Virginia didn't belong in the dark, and after spending a large chunk of her life in that damn windowless room, I was gonna make sure she had windows. Open space. A place that made her happy.

The building took a little longer to renovate than I'd hoped, but it was a hellhole, so I couldn't really expect anything less. It cost a small fortune, even if this was the ghetto. But everything was up to code, state of the art, and wheelchair friendly. Even the kitchen countertops were slightly lower so she could do all the baking she wanted.

And she did.

She was terrible at it.

I ate her bad cooking anyway and told her I liked it. I might be an asshole, but I wasn't mean.

Okay, I was mean. But not to my girl.

She'd get better after more practice. At least, I hoped. If she didn't, I'd have eternal acid reflux to go with my eternal Christmas celebrations.

Joy to the world.

I wanted to paint the walls in this place black. She wanted sunshine yellow. We settled on white. The floors were light-colored wood, almost gray, and the kitchen cabinets were white too. The island was black, though, but topped with a white stone countertop.

Green garland, wrapped with lights and jammed with glittery silver and gold ornaments, draped all around the island. Hell, the shit was draped everywhere. She even covered the sectional with pillows covered in snowflakes.

I told her we didn't need them. She threw them at me.

Stockings hung on the white fireplace mantel (which also was covered in garland), and they had our names on them. Including Snort and Zilla. White lights lined the windows, and a huge flower arrangement was in the center of the coffee table.

Snort went to his water bowl, sucked down about half, and then drooled a quarter of it all over the floor on the way to the big dog bed lying by the couch.

"Well?" Virginia called, drawing my attention.

"What?"

"What am I supposed to wear?"

"Why would I care? Wear what you want."

She tossed her hands up in the air. "But what if I wear sweatpants and it's somewhere fancy?"

I rolled my eyes. "I don't go to fancy places, and you hardly ever wear sweatpants."

She muttered something beneath her breath but then recovered to smile sweetly.

Shit.

"Fine. I'll wear that little sequined dress Ivory sent me." She spun on her wheels and took off down the hallway to the bedroom. On her way, she called, "That seems Christmas-y, and you said this was a Christmas surprise."

This woman was a damn menace.

My boots stomped back along the hall after her, going into the bedroom, which was painted a medium-tone gray. A color I actually liked. But then she moved in a giant cream-colored headboard made of velvet. And added more pillows than any person could ever need on the bed.

She looked tiny in the center and sank into it all like she was being swallowed by a cloud. It was kind of cute. Then she blew me. So yeah, the bed was pretty nice.

A low rumble vibrated my throat when I saw her reach into the closet and pull out that damn dress. I swear Ivory sent it over to drive me insane.

Stalking over, I plucked the red number from V's hands and tossed it onto the floor.

"Earth! It will get ruined."

"Good."

"That's what I'm wearing!"

"The hell you are. You know how I feel about that sack of sin."

She laughed. "Sack of sin?" she echoed, then laughed all over again.

I couldn't help it. I smiled.

When she finally stifled her cute as hell giggles, she announced, "You don't want me to wear it 'cause you're jealous."

"You're damn right," I deadpanned. "Let me catch one man looking at those legs of yours," I threatened. "I'll kill him."

She made a sound, totally ignoring the threat. That's how I knew it was serious. "If anyone looks at my legs, it won't be because they like them."

Any jealousy I felt evaporated. Dropping down in front of her, I grasped her hands. "What's this I'm hearing?"

"You know it's true." Her voice was quiet, eyes latched to where our hands held. "The only thing people notice about my legs is that they don't work."

A strangled sound left my lips. "Look at me," I demanded.

Her eyes lifted. The insecurity in their depths reached out to me, practically clutching my heart and squeezing. "I'm not gonna sit here and lie to you, tell you that no one notices the chair or the fact you can't walk." I began. "But I can also say with absolute certainty it's not the only thing people notice. In fact, the second they actually look at you, that chair becomes an afterthought."

I saw the denial form on her tongue, her kissable lips parting to argue against my words. I shook my head, cutting off whatever she would come up with.

"You know damn well I watch everything. Every detail when we're in a room. And I'm telling you I see how you affect people, sprite. You're goddamn beautiful. You sparkle like that glitter you love so much. Hell, you're the only one who's ever made my cold heart warm." Reaching up, I tucked a loose strand of hair behind her ear. "Why do you think I hate that dress so much? 'Cause I know it will draw all the eyes. I don't share, sprite, and you told me I couldn't be violent at Christmas."

Her lower lip trembled just slightly, but I saw and reached out to stroke my thumb over it. Puckering her lips, she kissed it. "You're the only one who's ever made me feel beautiful."

My heart slowed to a thud, its beat echoing between

my ears. "I'm a selfish bastard, V, so that makes me very happy."

"I should get changed." Her mouth brushed over my thumb with her whisper.

The featherlight caress made my groin tighten and need spike in my veins. "Okay," I said, reluctantly pulling away.

She caught my hand. "Earth?"

"Hmm?"

"Can you help me undress?" Releasing my hand, she lifted her arms.

Our eyes met when my hands slipped beneath the hem of the Christmas sweater she was wearing. Her breath quickened when I dragged the fabric up over her head and peeled it off her arms.

Her hair was mussed when I tossed the shirt aside, and the way she looked up from behind her thick lashes was foreplay all its own.

"I need help with this too." She beckoned, running a finger along the strap of her bra.

It was a front clasp she could take off all on her own, but if she said she needed help, then who was I to deny her?

I didn't bother crouching in front of her again. Instead, I moved in, letting her see the bulge against my black jeans. The pink tip of her tongue swiped over her lower lip as I filled her line of vision, reaching down to unclasp the bra with one hand.

The second the fabric opened, I peeled it back, revealing her perky little breasts. The nipples were already puckered, and I plucked at one, making her gasp.

Her body arched into that brief touch, so I filled both my hands with her chest, caressing and teasing her taut nipples. Small, quivering hands reached for the button on my jeans, and I shifted, practically straddling her legs.

I hissed a breath when my hard cock sprang free, practically falling out of my clothes in her direction. Arching into my busy hands, she reached for me, circling her hand around the head and stroking down.

My hands stalled out, falling to my sides as she stroked me again. Leaning close, she swiped her warm tongue over the tip like I was some kind of ice cream cone.

I moaned, and she wrapped her lips around me to suck.

The end of my shirt and my jacket got in her way, and she pushed at the fabric while trying to take more.

Ripping the fabric off my body, I thrust my hips in, making us both groan. She hummed, and the vibration of the sound made my dick jerk against the roof of her mouth.

Curling her hands around my hips, she held on, using me as an anchor as her head bobbed and moved. Her mouth was wet and warm, sheathing me in the kind of pleasure that made everything else in life disappear.

The strands of her hair tangled around my fingers when I pushed them into the thick mass and massaged her scalp. She hummed around me again, and I shuddered. She drew back and then plunged down again, taking me so deep I felt my tip bump the back of her throat. Instead of surging back, she stopped, holding herself still, holding my dick deep.

My stomach muscles tightened when she pulled back, slowly, lips grabbing on to every inch as she went until she swirled her tongue around the tip and pushed my jeans down my legs.

The second my clothes were gone, I lifted her out of

her chair, taking her to our cloudlike king-size bed. Laying her across, I stripped away her shoes, socks, and jeans. When she was completely bare, I let my eyes caress her body, letting her feel the heat of my desire.

"You are so beautiful," I told her.

She made a soft sound, and my body covered hers. The feel of her hard nipples rubbing over my chest made me kiss her a little harder. Impatient, I kissed across her jaw and dove into her neck. She arched up immediately, and I scraped my teeth over a particularly sensitive spot beneath her ear.

I was so attuned to her body now I practically felt her turn liquid with pleasure, and I nibbled at the spot again. Moving restlessly, her hands corded through my hair, holding me against her but also pushing down.

Chuckling, I moved, knowing what she wanted.

Her small moan rose to the ceiling when I latched onto her breast and sucked. All the muscles in her body tightened, vibrating with pleasure and need. I sucked a little deeper, and she whispered my name.

Still sucking, I reached for the other breast, rolling the nipple between two fingers. When her breathing was uneven and her chest was flushed, I trailed wet kisses down her stomach, delving my tongue instantly into her belly button. She arched up with a satisfied sigh.

Her belly button was an erogenous zone, as was her entire waistline right above her injury. So as I licked and sucked, I delved a hand between her legs, giving a satisfied groan when I felt how wet she was for me.

Pulling my hand up, I smeared her silky heat over her waist before pulling up. Her gaze was unfocused and her cheeks were pink when she looked at me.

Standing at the side of the bed, I hooked my hands beneath her knees, dragging her body over the mattress until her ass was practically hanging off. Lifting her legs, I put them on my shoulders.

"I want these beautiful stems on me," I murmured, stroking my palms down their smooth, soft length. "I want you to see them while I fuck you."

Her hair was spread out on the bed, her lips swollen, breasts flushed. And her flat stomach was slightly glossy from the way I'd been going at it.

Keeping hold of her legs with one arm, I grasped her hand and pressed it against her lower belly. "Feel me enter you," I said, then pushed in.

We both moaned. She was always so slick and tight. Being inside her was literally like nothing else I'd ever experienced. Her body welcomed me every time, and even though sometimes she didn't climax, there was always this state of bliss written across her face.

Leaving her hand against her stomach, I grabbed both legs and started to move. God, the way she looked laid out on the bed with me standing over her like this. Her breasts bounced with every thrust, and her breathing was heavy.

I started pounding faster, and her eyes slipped shut.

"Look at me," I said, thrusting deep.

Her eyes flickered, and I rubbed my hands over her legs. "Look how beautiful you are draped over me."

Her hand slipped from her stomach, but her eyes stayed on me.

"Touch yourself," I said, rough, my thrusts becoming a bit sloppy.

Her hands lifted to her breasts, fingers pinching and rolling the nipples. One of my hands covered her stomach, and I dipped a finger into her belly button. At the same moment, I thrust deep. So deep spots swam before my eyes. Gripping her legs against my chest, I pushed a little harder into her belly and rotated my hips.

The orgasm ripped over me like a tidal wave, crashing over every sense I had, pulling me down and slamming into me almost roughly. I spilled into her with a shout, feeling my dick throb and pulse as it emptied.

Her hand slapped over mine, and she moaned, body going slack into the blankets. My cock continued to pulse for a few minutes more, little aftershocks making me gasp as I hugged her legs against my torso.

When the intensity of the orgasm finally relaxed, I leaned down and kissed her ankle.

She smiled, and my heart warmed knowing even if she didn't feel the kiss, she saw it.

Lowering her legs, I slipped my arms under her body, pulling her chest flush against mine. "I love you."

She smiled. "I love you too."

"Don't go anywhere," I called over my shoulder as I went into the bathroom for a warm cloth.

"Har-har," she yelled back.

Once we were both cleaned up and she was sitting on the bed, I backtracked across the room to pick up the red sequined dress.

"Here." My voice was soft as I carried it over. "You should wear this."

"You want me to wear a *sack of sin*?" She pressed a hand to her chest as if I'd suggested something unthinkable.

I glowered. "Put it on. We're going to be late."

"But you said—"

"I know what I said. But I can handle a little jealousy."

"No. You can't."

I pretended like I didn't hear that. "Wear it and know

that every eye that looks your way tonight isn't looking at that chair. They're seeing how gorgeous you are."

She sniffled.

I recoiled. "Don't start crying. I don't like it."

She sniffled again.

I thrust the dress into her lap. "You don't want to miss your surprise, do you?"

Just like that, all threat of tears vanished. "Why are you just standing around naked? Hurry and get dressed!"

"You're lucky I love you," I bickered on my way to the closet to pull out my favorite: black jeans and a long-sleeved T-shirt.

"Wear the Christmas sweater I got you."

"No."

"Pleeease?"

Fuck.

I pulled on the hideous red and white sweater. It had fucking deer on it. Grimacing, I shrugged into my leather jacket, trying to cover up as much as possible.

"Can you help me?"

I turned, all thoughts of how personally victimized I felt wearing this ball of yarn disappearing. She was still sitting on the bed, legs draped over the edge. The red sequin dress was pulled down over her body, riding up high on her creamy thighs. The neckline was in the shape of a V, and it didn't have sleeves.

My girl being the braid whiz she was had her hair braided and pinned up at the back of her head, revealing the long column of her neck. There was a light mark just under her ear from my lips, but I didn't point it out because I didn't want her to cover it up.

"It needs zipped," she said when I just stood there staring.

When I leaned around her to grasp the zipper, I

breathed in deep, catching my scent still clinging to her skin. Satisfaction welled up in my chest as I zipped the dress around her.

I lifted her so she could pull the hem down and then helped her into her wheelchair. She went to the closet to pull out a pair of panties and some red shoes with small heels.

While she was in the bathroom, I strapped my blade to my back beneath my jacket. With the way she was looking tonight, I'd probably need it.

"Do I look okay?" she asked, wheeling back into the room.

She was a small woman, but damn, if it didn't feel like her legs were a mile long. Probably because the dress was short and showed more of her legs than I was used to.

I seriously wanted to tell her to put on some pants. But I thought about her words earlier, and I bit my tongue. Just because she was paralyzed didn't mean she wasn't gorgeous. It didn't mean her legs should be hidden. And it sure as hell didn't mean that people would look over her beauty because of her disability.

Fuck that.

But if anyone touched her, they were dead.

"You look like I might do some jail time."

"I'm being serious, Earth!"

"So am I," I deadpanned. Lowering before her, I grasped her chin, making it so our eyes collided. "You are literally the most beautiful thing I have ever seen."

"Thank you."

"Come on." My voice was gruff. "Get your coat. We have to go."

"Where are we going again?"

Cheeky. "Nice try," I said, reaching into the closet.

"But you'll find out when we get there." I draped an over-sized scarf over her legs.

She gave me a look.

"What?" I said. "It's cold out."

She laughed.

"Come on," I called, leaving the bedroom. "I'm leaving without you!"

She gasped. "You wouldn't!"

She was right. I wouldn't.

8

VIRGINIA

"REALLY!" I PRACTICALLY SQUEALED THE SECOND THE CAB pulled to a stop.

"Want me to get closer?" the cabbie called back to where we sat.

"No. This is good," Earth replied.

Nose still pressed against the window, I took in the grand red, blue, and yellow lights. "That tree is huge!" I exclaimed. "Earth, do you see?"

"I'd have to be blind not to."

"You aren't even looking!" I said, grabbing a fistful of his jacket and pulling him toward the window. He came, fitting his chin against my shoulder.

"I've seen the Radio City Music Hall before, sprite." His voice rumbled against my ear. "Pretty sure you have too."

"But never lit up like this at night! And at Christmas!"

Oh, it was so beautiful. There was this certain magic that just radiated Christmas spirit.

I could feel his even breathing brushing my cheek, and little prickles of awareness scattered over my scalp and raced down my neck. I glanced over my shoulder at him. "Is this really where we're going?"

"Haven't you always wanted to see the Christmas Spectacular?"

My vision turned blurry with the sudden rush of tears. "I've always wanted to see the Rockettes."

He smiled. "Surprise."

Forgetting the view, I threw my arms around his neck, hugging him tight. "Thank you."

"You should feel guilty for making me wear this heinous sweater," he quipped.

"How could I feel guilty? Look how cute you are!" I looked at the cab driver. "Isn't he cute?"

A beat of awkward silence.

"I like women, ma'am," he said awkwardly.

I burst out laughing, and Earth handed him a wad of cash before lifting me out of the back and into my chair.

Radio City Music Hall sat on the corner of the block, the huge sign lighting up everything in close range. The giant Christmas tree sitting on the sign had to have thousands of lights and reached up toward the sky just like all the buildings.

"It's so pretty," I said, gazing up.

"I should have brought my sunglasses," Earth grumped.

The night air was cold, so cold that I could feel it partway down my throat when I breathed in, and white puffs bloomed in front of my mouth when I exhaled. I stared at the glittering sign a few moments longer, watching the words *Christmas Spectacular - The Rockettes* scrolling along the lower portion of the sign practically wrapping around the building.

I'd only ever seen the Rockettes perform on television and online. They were so incredibly talented, and their costumes were so elaborate. I knew they changed many times throughout the show, and I always wanted to experience it in person at the theater.

And now I could.

I reached for Earth's hand, bringing it to my face to nuzzle against it.

"Ready to go in?" he asked, brushing against my cheek one last time.

"Is it wheelchair accessible?" I worried.

"Yes, sweetheart," he said, pushing me under the large awning. "Even if it wasn't, I'd just carry you in."

I sniffled. For so long, I'd felt like I'd never be able to do anything I wanted to do. Just leaving the Tower seemed like a grand adventure. It seemed unbelievable I didn't even live there anymore and that grumpy old Earth was willing—no, he wanted—to take me all the places I'd always longed to go.

There was a line stretching around the building, but Earth ignored it, pushing me right to the door.

"Earth! You can't just cut the line!" I scolded him.

A few people nearby snickered.

"We have VIP tickets." His voice was dry. "We get to go in first."

"Of course," I said, settling back into the chair. People who needed special assistance getting inside usually did go in first.

The door to inside opened, and a man wearing a very classy outfit stepped out, holding it open. "Welcome to the Christmas Spectacular!" he said. "We are so glad to have you as a guest this evening."

I started to reach out my hand to greet him properly, but my chair jolted to a stop, and Earth's jean-clad, leather-wearing self stepped in front of me.

"What are you doing?" I asked.

"Let's get something straight," he said, crouching down in front of me so we were eye level.

I knew that look. I wasn't moving from this spot until he said whatever it was he needed to say. Leaning around him, I glanced at the concierge. "I'm terribly sorry. One moment please."

He inclined his head. "Of course."

I looked at Earth once more. "Yes?"

His near-black eyes softened a bit as they swept my face. "Even if you weren't on wheels, we'd still be going in before anyone else. I bought VIP tickets, which are available to anyone, not just people who need assistance."

I blinked. "Did I say that out loud?" I wondered.

"You don't have to say anything at all, sweetheart. I know what goes on in that head of yours."

I threw my arms around him, making him rock a little into his heels, but he caught me and steadied us both. His arms wrapped tight around my torso, hugging me close.

"Merry Christmas, baby," he whispered.

I will not cry, I told myself. Pulling back, I pressed a kiss to his lips, which were cold from the air. "Can we go inside now?"

"Beats standing on the sidewalk."

The man in the dapper uniform smiled when we approached, still holding open the door.

"Hello, sir! I love your suit. You look very handsome."

Behind me, Earth made a sound.

"Madam." The man took my hand and bowed over it. "I hope you enjoy the show."

Earth didn't even give me a chance to respond. Instead, he forged ahead, pushing the chair through the doors into the lobby.

"That was so rude," I hissed over my shoulder.

"I'd never wear that getup he had on."

I rolled my eyes.

Once we made it through the lobby, we made our way into the grand foyer, which was exactly that: grand.

I sat up straighter in the chair, widening my eyes so I could take in as much as possible. "Oh my goodness!" I exclaimed. "This is more beautiful than I ever imagined."

I didn't know where to look first! There were huge lit wreaths along the walls, which were a rich golden-brown color that matched the lighted, grand green garlands that draped every level of the tall interior. Vendors lined the walls, offering snacks and mementos. All of their little stations were decorated for Christmas too. The carpet was lavish with some sort of golden pattern, and the ceilings were so tall!

But the centerpiece of it all was what kept drawing my awe.

"I've never seen such an elaborate and beautiful chandelier in all my life."

"It's ludicrous," Earth declared.

I gasped. "It is not! Just look!" I said, pointing at the oversized golden chandelier, which managed to fill the massively high ceilings. It was draped in crystals, warm lights, and shaped expertly to look like the most luxurious Christmas tree ever made. It made me think of a million glimmering stars.

Earth made a sound. "I guess it's all right."

Huge mirrors were hung on the walls, which reflected the light back into the room, making everything glow.

"Do you want anything from out here?" he asked, drawing my eyes back to the vendors. Even though we were early to come inside, there were others in here as well, mingling around, purchasing items, and gazing at the decorations.

"Can we look around a bit before we go to our seats?"

"We can do whatever you want, sprite."

We explored the grand foyer, looking at all the trees and decorations, and then rode the elevator to some of the higher levels to look at even more beautiful trees and lights. On each level, the chandelier looked even more beautiful than the last.

At some point during our exploration, I tugged off my coat and the scarf draped over my legs. "Oh, look!" I exclaimed, pointing. "More trees!"

"If you've seen one tree, you've seen them all," Mr. Grumpy-grump declared, but he pushed me gently in the direction I wanted to go.

This display was near the restrooms, and a woman wearing a lovely green dress came out, and I waved at her. "Excuse me, ma'am? Would you mind taking our picture?"

Earth made a rough sound. "I'll take it."

"You're going to be in it."

He looked like he was about to protest, but I grasped his hand and batted my eyes. "I want to remember this night forever."

"All right, sweetheart." He relented, handing the woman his cell phone.

Instead of pushing the chair in front of the trees, he swept me up into his arms, making me laugh. Automatically, my arms looped around his neck.

"Smile!" the woman said, holding up the phone.

He made a strangled noise, and I tickled the back of his neck. "Just a little smile?"

His lips curved up, and I beamed.

"You two make such a beautiful couple," the woman said, returning the phone to Earth. "And that dress is absolutely beautiful on you."

"Thank you very much," I said, my cheeks feeling warm.

"Happy?" Earth asked when she was gone.

"So happy."

"I have to piss," he announced.

"Earth!"

He rolled his eyes. "Excuse me, milady. I need to use the gentlemen's facilities. Will you be okay here by the trees while I go?"

I giggled. "You can talk like a gentleman!"

He made a face. "I've been hanging around Ethan too long."

"Go on. I'll be here."

He hesitated. "Do you need to go?"

I shook my head. "No. I'm good."

He hesitated again.

"For goodness sakes, Earth. I'm perfectly capable of waiting for you while you go to the bathroom."

He nodded, leaned down, and kissed the top of my head. "Be right back."

Once his leather-clad frame disappeared into the men's room, I rotated back toward the railing overlooking the grand foyer. The chandelier really was spectacular.

I was studying how the gold chains covered in crystals and lights were hung perfectly to mimic the shape of a tree when someone moved up beside me.

I smiled. "That was fast," I said, still gazing over the

foyer. "How long do you think it takes them to decorate all of this?"

"More time than I have."

I jolted, rotating to see the man beside me. The man who was not Earth.

"Oh! I thought you were someone else," I said, pressing a hand to my chest.

He chuckled warmly. He was tall, dressed in dress pants and a dress shirt. He wore a long wool coat and had a scarf draped around his neck. His hair was short around the sides and combed back on the top. He was probably around thirty and had green eyes.

"I didn't mean to startle you. I just saw something beautiful and had to take a closer look."

"Well, this chandelier is quite beautiful." I agreed, turning back to it.

"I wasn't talking about the light."

It took a moment for his words to register, and when they did, I gazed back at him, confused.

He chuckled again, a dimple appearing in his cheek. "Oh, come now, you can't be that startled to have someone call you beautiful. Surely, you hear it all the time."

"Well, yes," I mumbled, not sure what to say. I mean, Earth told me all the time, and my family said so, but this was completely different. Wasn't it?

"I think red must be your color."

I felt myself blush. "Thank you."

"Of course, a beauty like you probably looks good in every color."

Is this man flirting with me? Never in all my life had anyone ever just approached and started flirting.

"Are you here with a friend?" He continued, clearly not noticing my shock.

"Who the fuck are you?" Earth's voice was calm and quiet, but it radiated with unspoken intensity.

Stiffening, the man turned to look over his shoulder at Earth. "Hello. And you are?"

"About to make your life a living hell."

"Earth!" I gasped.

The man turned back to me. "Do you know this person?"

"He's my boyfriend," I said immediately.

Shock widened the man's eyes. "Him?"

"Yeah. Me. So you better put your eyes back in your head before I—"

I cut off Earth's threat with some of my own. "Yes, of course. I love him very much. Now, if you will excuse me, we have to get to our seats. I hope you enjoy the show."

"I don't," Earth deadpanned.

I didn't even bother to tell him he was rude. He already knew.

"I leave you alone for five minutes..." Earth glowered as we waited for the elevator. Crossing his arms over his chest, he looked me up and down. "What did he say to you?"

"Nothing."

"Virginia."

"He just told me I was beautiful."

"And?"

"And that red was a good color for me."

"That sack of sin," he muttered. "Drawing in the pervs from all over." The elevator opened, and we moved into the car. "Good thing I brought my blade."

My mouth dropped open. "You did not!"

He lifted his jacket to show me the harness.

"How dare you strap that over that Christmas sweater?"

"I wouldn't have to if you weren't rolling around looking like that."

"You told me to wear it!"

He made a face like he was constipated. "Because I wanted you to know how beautiful you are. Not just to me but to everyone else too."

"I didn't flirt back." I rebuked.

He grunted. "Do you believe me now?"

"I always believe everything you say."

He chuckled under his breath. The elevator dinged open, revealing the grand foyer once more. It was filling up fast, the large space crowding with guests. Seeing them all made me pause for a moment, my chair stalling out.

Noting the reaction, Earth stepped in front of me like a shield. "What is it?"

"Nothing," I said, secretly thinking how sweet the gesture was. Even if he was a big jerk sometimes. "It's just getting so busy!"

The doors started to close, and he stuck his boot between them, making them open anew.

Turning back, he leaned down, caging me in with his arms, hovering just above me. "Let's head to our seats before someone else tries to flirt with you and I get in a fight."

"I don't want to flirt with anyone but you."

He kissed me.

It didn't take long to make it to our seats, which were on the orchestra level, the very first level closest to the stage! They were fantastic! Apparently, the very best seats were in the middle, so that's what he reserved. The staff allowed us to leave my chair off to the side, and

Earth carried me into the middle section, placing me in my seat.

Tears filled my eyes when he placed me down, and I gazed up at the huge stage draped in heavy curtains. The ceiling above the stage was arched and glowed with different levels of lights. The seats were red velvet and felt soft under my fingertips.

"Is this seat okay?" he asked, settling beside me. "Are you comfortable? If your chair is more comfortable, we can move."

"No," I said, grasping his forearm. "This is perfect."

"Hey," he said, turning his body toward mine. His knees bumped my legs, and he put his hands on my upper body to make up for the fact I couldn't feel the touch. "What's these tears?"

"I'm just so happy. This theater is so amazing. And to get to sit here in a seat that isn't even my chair… It's even more than I hoped for."

His whole face softened, showing me a side of him that only I ever got to see. The pad of his thumb was slightly rough as it brushed away my tears. "We're going to see lots more shows and do all the stuff you've always wanted to do."

"I love you." I gasped and hurried to add, "But not because of this! I'd love you even if we didn't do anything at all!"

He laughed. I loved the sound of his laugh. "I know, sweetheart."

The Christmas Spectacular was named that for a very specific reason. Because it was totally spectacular. And the Rockettes! My gosh, they were so in sync. They moved like they were one body. They never missed a beat, and those high kicks! And their costumes! So elaborate and beautiful!

My favorite part was when they dressed as toy soldiers and when Santa came out at the end. There was even a small ice skating rink that had people skating on it as part of the show. Even Earth was impressed, though he pretended not to be. By the time the curtain went down and the music went out, my face hurt from smiling so much.

And my hands! They stung from all the clapping.

"Well?" Earth asked as we remained seated while others were filing out. "How was your first Rockette show?"

I burst into tears.

Alarmed, Earth pulled me into his lap, cradling me close. I pushed his jacket out of the way and rubbed my nose on his sweater.

"Snot will probably make this thing look better," he mused.

I laughed in the middle of crying.

He let me cry it out, let me wipe more tears on his shirt (which he called snot—so gross), and I heard him tell a few people over my head I was fine, just happy. He wasn't even mean to them.

Finally, I lifted my face, swiping the back of my hand over my cheek. "I'm sorry."

He smiled. "Don't be sorry, sprite. I'm glad you had a good time."

"Did you?" I asked.

I saw the denial form on his tongue, but then he swallowed, and a warm look came into his eyes. "Yeah, I did. It wasn't as terrible as I thought."

"We can come again?"

"Don't push your luck."

I giggled.

Reaching between us, he grasped my chin and pulled

my face up. "I'll bring you back here anytime you want, okay?"

I nodded.

"C'mon, then," he said, standing up, bringing me with him. "Let's stop and get some hot chocolate on the way home. Maybe swing by and see the tree at Rockefeller Center."

"I thought you said if you've seen one tree, you've seen them all," I teased.

"You can look at the tree, and I'll look at you."

I smiled. *Such a softie inside.*

It didn't matter how many more shows Earth and I went to see. This was our first, and it was during our first Christmas in love. And because of that, it would forever be my favorite.

9

IVORY

LYING IS A DEPLORABLE HABIT. I REALLY DID MY BEST TO BE as straightforward as possible. I would much rather have someone give it to me straight rather than hear a bunch of falsehoods.

Wouldn't you agree?

Alas, I lived with Neo, who lied better than some people dressed. Naturally, I picked up a thing or two. About lying. I already knew how to dress. Even if I was currently wrapped up in an unfortunate red plaid flannel, which just made me look like the liar I was not.

Except for this morning. This morning, I was filled with lies. It made me feel horribly guilty.

But sometimes a girl had to do what a girl had to do. And sometimes a lie was less scary than the truth.

A sleepy sound filled the bedroom when Neo rolled toward me, his body sliding close beneath the blankets. His arm wound around my waist, and another sound vibrated his throat. My body fit seamlessly against his, and he nuzzled my neck.

"Aren't you usually gone for a run by now?" His voice was husky from sleep, making my heart flutter.

"I wanted to stay in bed with you," I murmured, rubbing my palm up and down his bicep.

That was my first lie.

I mean, technically, it wasn't a lie. I would much rather stay in bed with Neo than go running in Central Park. However, this wasn't the reason I was still in bed.

"Hmm," he mused, sliding his leg in between mine. "Is that so?"

The arm thrown over my body pulled back so his hand could drag over my midsection. Lifting my chin, I exposed the column of my neck, and he pressed his lips against it. I made a sound of pleasure, arching up a little, and his hand started to move. Neo's strong, artist hand slid under the flannel, gliding over bare skin and leaving chills in its wake. His wide palm covered my entire breast, squeezing lightly, and a needy moan dropped into the room.

"Sensitive this morning," he murmured, latching onto my neck again.

I pushed my breast up into his hand as he massaged, pinching the nipple and making me cry out.

Cool air brushed over the wetness left behind on my neck when he pulled back, rolling over me so he was settled between my spread thighs.

The bedroom was still dim because the curtains were drawn, but I felt the intensity of his stare even in the shadows. Deft fingers made short work of the buttons on the flannel, and he opened it quickly, revealing my entire naked torso.

Without wasting time, he latched onto one breast,

sucking gently. Pushing my fingers into his hair, I pressed him harder against me, asking for more. Grasping my breasts in his hands, he held them and went harder. Moaning, I felt my core grow slick, and I began to squirm restlessly against the sheets.

When both my breasts were saturated with his attention, he clamped his fingers around the puckered nipples and slipped down my body, nibbling my flesh as he went.

"Open wider for me, princess," he said, nudging the apex of my thighs with his nose.

I did, but he made a sound, releasing the pinching pressure he'd been applying to my nipples. I cried out at the loss of sensation as two hands spanned my inner thighs and pushed. He spread my legs so wide I was utterly exposed and vulnerable.

"You're already dripping."

"Please, Neo," I whispered, reaching down toward my core. "I need you."

When he shoved down the waistband of his boxers, his hard cock jutted between us proudly. Not bothering to strip them completely, he moved into position and thrust.

The same moment he went deep, his teeth scraped over my nipple, and a low keening sound floated above us.

Grunting in satisfaction, his palms hit the mattress on either side of me, and he pulled out, thrusting back in without pause. My nails dug into his biceps as I tilted my hips and held on. He pumped into me relentlessly, giving exactly what I needed. My whole world condensed into nothing but the sensation of being speared by him over and over again.

Bliss emptied my head, and pleasure was all I knew. It built and built until I needed even more. Releasing his arms, I reached around to grab his ass, pulling him deep. Over me, he shuddered, and inside me, he throbbed. Arching into him, my mouth fell open and my world fell apart. His release prolonged mine, my body hungrily milking every last drop he had to give. Eventually, I went boneless against the mattress, feeling satiated and comforted in a way I didn't even know I needed.

Supporting his weight on his arms, he leaned down, capturing my lips in a lazy, sloppy kiss. "I like when you skip your runs."

I giggled. "Tell me that when I get fat!"

Smiling his crooked smile, he pulled back, dark locks of hair falling into his eyes. "Sweetheart, the only kind of fat you will ever be is P-H-A-T."

I wrinkled my nose. "Is that some kind of Grimms speak?"

He widened his eyes. "What's this? Did I finally find a word Ms. Ivory White does not know?"

I rolled my eyes. "It's probably not even a word."

"It means crazy sexy. So sexy you're phat with it."

"That's not even a compliment." I sniffed.

He leaned in, the universe in his endless gaze sparkling. "Wanna take a shower?"

I pursed my lips, pretending to think it over.

His eyebrows wagged. "I'll wash your back."

"Deal!"

With a whoop, he bounded out of bed. Everything he did always held so much animation. "Come on," he said, wrapping his hand around my ankle to pull.

I shrieked, gripping for the covers as I was so rudely dragged to the side of the bed. "Neo!"

I was half hanging off the bed when he let go, my legs sagging toward the floor. Before I could stand, he came over me, our chests nearly brushing. "Don't you trust me?"

I smiled. "Always."

Grasping my hands, he towed me up onto my feet. A dizzy spell knocked into me, making me sway.

"Whoa," he intoned, hands coming back to steady me. Concern darkened his face as he studied me. "Are you sick?" he asked, pressing a hand against my forehead. Before I could answer, he went rigid. "If you aren't feeling well, why the hell did you let me go at you like that?"

"Oh, for heaven's sake! I'm fine. I missed dinner last night, so I'm a little dizzy is all."

"Why the hell didn't you eat?" he demanded.

"I'm not speaking to you until you can use a respectable tone." I reprimanded, pulling away to pad toward the bathroom.

He rushed after me, slipping an arm around my waist. "Let's eat before we shower."

My stomach turned. "I can't possibly enjoy my breakfast while I'm filthy."

"Such a princess," he muttered. "You aren't even dirty."

"Between my legs begs to differ."

"I like it when you talk dirty to me," he growled. I gasped when he swept me up into his arms, carrying me the rest of the way into the bathroom. "Tell me, princess. What's it like still feeling me between your thighs?"

I blushed.

His chuckle was throaty and arrogant.

He was an absolute caveman.

After our shower, I dressed in a white cashmere turtleneck and a pair of cream-colored trousers that were cuffed at the ankles. Still in my walk-in closet, I crept to the door like I was some kind of criminal and peered out.

Neo was making a racket in the kitchen—honestly, he never did anything quietly—so I tiptoed back and grabbed my phone. My manicured nails tapped the screen quickly as I sent off a text message.

This is Ivory White. Would it be possible to meet you at your office?

Once it was sent, I gazed around guiltily like I was doing something wrong. *This does not count as a lie.* I assured myself.

Spoiler alert: If you have to convince yourself you aren't lying… you are.

I waited around for what felt like an incredible amount of time, but no reply came. No longer able to procrastinate, I slipped the phone into my pocket and left the closet.

My white Dolce and Gabbana heels clipped sharply over the floor on the way to the kitchen as I gazed at all our beautiful holiday decorations. This year, we decorated in tones of white and red. The whole penthouse looked like a snow castle with pops of vibrant red. The trees were all flocked and adorned with white and red ornaments made of sequins, crystal, and glass. Virginia created us beautiful matching flower bouquets arranged in tall crystal vases and filled with bright cranberries.

Frosted wreaths bursting with holly berries adorned the kitchen, and handmade red velvet stockings hung on the mantel, which was topped with tall cone-shaped trees made out of white faux fur. I purchased one stocking for everyone in our big family, so they lined the entire shelf.

Neo was at the cooktop scrambling eggs with a plate

of bacon at his elbow. When he saw me, he smiled. "Almost ready, sweetheart."

I wrinkled my nose. "I'm not eating that."

"But, sweetheart, you're so hungry, so I made this nice meal for you."

I paused on my way to the espresso maker. I really didn't want to be rude. I'd already lied once today. *Okay, maybe twice.* "How very kind of you. Thank you for thinking of me."

"So you'll eat it?"

I blanched.

He threw back his head and laughed. Abandoning the pan, he caught me around the waist and pulled me close. "I know you don't like scrambled eggs and bacon, princess."

"Honestly, Neo, I was beginning to wonder if you listen to anything I say!" I demanded.

An ornery twinkle lit up his galaxy eyes. "You're so easy to tease."

I turned my face away. "I don't even know why I put up with you."

"Because I love you," he whispered, rotating me away from the espresso machine toward the island. "I already made your fancy coffee. Just the way you like it."

There next to the giant hand-poured cinnamon-scented candle was my latte. "You made that for me?"

He patted my butt and pushed me toward it, but I spun, suddenly emotional, and hugged him. "Thank you, Neo."

He grunted. "It's just coffee."

I sniffled into his shoulder, breathing in his scent. "But I appreciate it."

"My eggs are gonna burn." His voice was gruff.

"Then they'll smell worse than they already do."

We settled at the marble-topped island, Neo with his plate of eggs and bacon and me with my coffee, some organic yogurt, and granola.

I was pushing it around the bowl when I felt Neo's stare.

"What?" I asked, fearing I'd been caught.

"Why are you dressed like that?"

How rude! "And what is wrong with this outfit?" Totally offended, I glanced down at the monochrome ensemble.

"It looks like something you'd wear to work."

"Well, I *am* going to work."

He frowned.

"Neo?" I questioned.

"It's not like you to forget things."

My stomach churned, and my mind raced. "What did I forget?"

"We were supposed to go get a tree from Fletcher today."

I gasped. "Oh my gosh!" I exclaimed. "That's today!"

Neo winced, covering his ear. "It's a miracle I'm not deaf by now."

Pulling my phone from my pocket, I pulled up my very organized and detailed calendar. It was there. *Tree day with Fletcher!*

Absolute horror befell me. A strangled sound ripped from my throat. I was still staring at the calendar when the reply I'd been so anxiously waiting for in the closet came through.

Of course. See you soon.

I burst into tears.

Neo's chair made a scraping sound over the floor when he shoved back. "It's all right now," he said, scooping me up to sit down with me in his lap. "It's nothing to cry about."

Pressing my cheek against his chest, I clutched the phone against mine. "I never forget anything," I wailed. "And something so important!"

"Shh." He soothed, stroking a hand over my sleek hair. "We can go tomorrow."

I jolted up so fast I probably would have slid off his lap if he hadn't caught me. "But it's his first day today. We're all supposed to go to support him."

"Can you reschedule your morning?" he asked, the calm to my chaos.

My fingers tightened around the phone I still held, and I sobbed anew.

"I guess that's a no?" he quipped.

"I have a really important meeting this morning. I really can't reschedule." *Lie number three.*

Pulling back from his chest, I felt my lower lip wobble. "I'm a horrible sister."

"You are not." Taking my face in between his hands, he kissed me softly. "Fletcher will understand, okay? Go to your meeting."

I hesitated, feeling torn. The urge to spill everything was so overwhelming I actually felt the words clawing up the back of my throat.

"Eyes on me," Neo commanded.

I looked up.

"What's the matter, sweetheart?"

Oh, that soft voice could undo me. "I feel so guilty."

His lips pressed against my forehead. "Don't feel guilty, baby. Everyone knows you're a busy woman. Shit happens. Besides, we have plans with Ethan and Fletcher tonight. You can see him then."

Oh my God! "I forgot about that too!" I wailed.

CAMBRIA HEBERT

He rubbed slow, soothing circles over my back until I calmed down and relaxed into him.

"What are we doing tonight?" I asked, feeling ridiculous because I didn't know that either.

"I'm not sure," he replied. "Ethan didn't tell me, just asked if we would want to do something with him and Fletch."

Oh. Well, at least I didn't forget that.

"I guess it will be okay since I will see Fletch tonight. I can apologize."

Neo made a reassuring sound. "Go to your meeting, princess. Everything will be fine."

I wondered if he knew about all my lies, would he still say that?

10

Neo

"Want me to drive you?" I asked, her hand wrapped in mine as we went down to the parking garage.

"My driver is already bringing the car around."

I made a rude sound. "So? I'll make him get out. If my princess wants me to drive her, then I'll drive her."

She smiled, leaning into my body as we walked. "I really love you."

My chest expanded hearing the words, as it did every time she said them. Even still, I gazed at her from the corner of my eye because something was off.

Ivory was a top-tier drama queen. I was used to my ears ringing on a regular basis. But this morning was different.

She wasn't just a drama queen. She was… *emotional*. And even though it was no big deal she'd forgotten our plans, it was unlike her.

"Big meeting this morning?" I asked, nonchalantly.

She was suddenly suspicious. "Why?"

I shrugged. "You seem kinda nervous."

"Being nervous for a meeting is unprofessional," she said coolly, her austere Upper East Side breeding wrapping around her like a shield.

Interesting.

"But it is important."

I nodded. "If you need me, you can call, okay?"

"Aren't you going to see Fletcher?"

"I wasn't sure if you would want me to."

Her fingers clutched mine. "Oh yes, Neo, you must! You know how excited he is to be working there again. Go support him and get us a tree."

"Are you sure?" I asked, searching her blue stare for any traces of doubt.

She nodded. "Absolutely certain. I'll try and come home early so we can decorate it together before we go out."

Her driver pulled to the curb in a black SUV with heavily tinted windows.

Stepping forward, I opened the door. "Your carriage awaits." But I didn't wait for her to come forward. Instead, my palms spanned her waist, and I lifted her easily into the vehicle.

Leaning in, I buckled the seat belt around her. "Hey." I spoke softly, pushing a strand of black hair off her cheek. "You can call if you need me."

She tried to hide the way her lower lip wobbled by pulling her bow-shaped mouth into a smile. "I know. I'll see you soon."

When I kissed her, her lips clung just a little longer than usual.

I stood there staring after the SUV long after it turned out of sight. Something was definitely going on.

11

Ivory

"So sorry to have kept you waiting," he said before he was even fully in the room.

I was wound so tight that just hearing his voice nearly made me snap. White-knuckling the chair armrests, I did my best to smile. "It's not a problem. Thank you for seeing me on such short notice."

"I'm always available for you," he said, perfectly poised and unruffled. Acting like the documents he held in his hand couldn't alter the rest of my life.

Confession: I didn't have a big meeting. I had a doctor's appointment. I forgot our family plans because I couldn't concentrate on anything else. I wouldn't be able to until I knew.

"Please," I said, trying to remain as composed as everyone knew me to be. "Just tell me."

"The test was positive. You're pregnant."

Falling back into the chair, I heaved out a shuddering breath. "Are you sure?"

"Quite. That's why you had to wait so long. I ran it twice. You are most definitely pregnant."

Tears filled my eyes, spilling over before I could even think about trying to blink them back. *A baby.* Mine and Neo's. *Our baby.*

I sniffled, more tears sliding down my cheeks.

"Ms. White." Dr. Selca said, coming close to my chair. "Are you all right?"

I put my hand to my stomach, completely lost to the fact that inside me right now was my son or daughter.

"I take it this is a surprise?"

"Oh, yes," I whispered, still focusing inward.

A throat cleared.

I glanced up. "What was that?"

"Is this a happy surprise?"

I gasped so strongly the doctor swayed back. "Oh yes!" I exclaimed, ferocity in my tone. "I could never be unhappy about this."

"Of course." He obliged. "Well, that's wonderful. Congratulations are in order."

"Thank you so much," I replied politely, then gasped once more.

"Is there something else?" he asked warily.

"I was—I *am* on birth control. How could this happen?" I asked. Then, "*Agh!*"

Dr. Selca jumped back. "My goodness. Should I call someone?"

"My baby!" I said, sitting forward. "I've been taking birth control! Is my baby okay?"

"Ah, yes. Your baby is fine. I see no reason to worry. Obviously, you will need to discontinue the medication immediately and switch it out for a quality prenatal vitamin—"

"Oh, please tell me the absolute best one. I'll get it right away," I said, cutting him off.

"Of course." He inclined his head. "I have every reason to believe you will take as excellent care of your baby as you do of yourself."

I gasped again.

"Ma'am," he said, pressing a hand to his chest. "I must ask that you please refrain from such behavior."

"I apologize," I said, even though I thought he was quite rude. How did he expect me to feel just finding out I was pregnant? We hadn't even been trying!

"While not usual, it is also not uncommon for women to get pregnant while on birth control. So as I said, just discontinue the medication, and all will be fine."

I nodded. "How far along am I? When am I due? Can I have a photo?"

"Slow down, slow down," he said, laughing a bit beneath his breath. "I forget how excited first-time mothers can be."

Oh my goodness, I'm going to be a mother.

Fresh tears welled in my eyes as I thought of my own mother, my baby's grandmother. I thought of how happy my father would be to have a new generation of our family. How I wished they could be here for this. How I wished my child could know them.

Even so, he or she will have plenty of family to love them.

A lump formed in my throat, emotion rising in me so fast I could barely swallow. A misfit baby. Oh, how wonderful. *They're going to be so happy.*

"Ms. White, are you listening?"

My head snapped up. "Oh! I'm so sorry. What were you saying?"

He smiled. "It's a lot to take in, isn't it?"

I nodded. "Yes, but I'm very happy." I didn't want him to think otherwise. Everyone would know how much I loved and wanted this baby.

He held a piece of paper across the desk to me. "Here's the name of the vitamins I recommend. I will have the script sent to your pharmacy electronically, but this is so you have the name written down. You can pick them up anytime this afternoon."

I nodded.

"As for everything else, why don't you make an appointment on your way out for next week? It will give you a little time for this to sink in. You and Neo can come in together, and we can see if we can hear the heartbeat, take an early ultrasound, and go over anything else you might be concerned about."

"Neo," I echoed, my heart squeezing.

I have a piece of Neo inside me.

Dr. Selca cleared his throat, and an awkward vibe suffused the room. "I do apologize. That was very forward of me. I just assumed Neo is, ah, was the father. You're a very well-known couple."

"He is!" I exclaimed, not even trying to control my voice. "Oh, of course he is!"

"Maybe I should offer him a hearing exam when he comes in," he muttered, rubbing his earlobe.

And he thought I was the dramatic one? I begged to differ.

"What was that?" I asked sweetly.

Alarmed, he cleared his throat. "Oh, nothing. So it's settled. Come in next week and bring Neo."

I swallowed, excitement still making my hands shake but also sensing the same worry plaguing me this morning.

"Dr. Selca?" I asked, rising to my feet.

"Yes?"

"How far along am I?"

"Well, according to the information you provided here on your paperwork, I would guess you are between six and eight weeks."

"And feeling nauseous is normal?"

"Yes, it's perfectly normal."

Without thinking, I placed my hand over my stomach. "Thank you so much."

"You're welcome. Congratulations again."

"Oh," I said before opening the door.

His face remained patient.

"Please don't tell anyone. I want to tell Neo."

"I would never," he informed, pert. "Doctor-patient confidentiality."

"Yes. Of course." I agreed. "Thank you again, you are a wonderful doctor. My baby is lucky to have you."

His face softened. "Have a nice day."

On my way out, I stopped at the desk and made an appointment. The entire time, my head swirled. A baby!

I couldn't be happier.

But what about Neo? Would he be happy too?

12

Neo

IT WAS AFTERNOON BY THE TIME I DRAGGED THE TREE ALL the way from the Grimms to the Upper East Side (one star, do not recommend) and got it set up and strung with white lights.

I figured having the lights done ahead of time would be a time-saver. And also, a sanity-saver. For all of her poise and grace, Ivory was also clumsy. She'd probably electrocute herself or set the place on fire if I handed her a set of string lights.

The entire time I worked, the back of my mind lingered on this morning. I couldn't shake the uneasy feeling I had.

The front door opened just as I reached for my cell to call her and check in. Tossing it down, I walked into the foyer.

I didn't see her at first, the large tree standing in the middle of the space blocking her small frame from sight.

But the second I stepped around it, my eyes found her right away.

She was leaning back against the closed door, holding her designer bag in front of her. She seemed a million miles away, not even noticing me.

"Princess? What's wrong?" I demanded, going right to her.

Her blue eyes widened, finally seeing me. "Oh! Neo."

Taking her bag, I tossed it onto the floor and tugged her to me. "Neo! That's a Balenciaga bag!"

"A ba-whatta?"

She smacked my arm. "You always say that."

"Then why do you bother telling me the designer?" I retorted.

She sighed sadly. "It really is a waste of my time."

"Hey." I spoke softly, catching her chin to angle her face up to mine. "Everything okay? How was the meeting?"

Her expression shifted just slightly, her eyes taking on a sheen, and then her fingers curled into the front of the flannel shirt I was wearing.

"Hey now," I crooned, worry filling me, and cupped her head, pushing her cheek into my chest. I hugged as tight as I dared, her fingers still clutching my shirt. Her head felt small in the palm of my hand, and my protective instincts roared to life.

"Neo," she whispered.

"Did something happen?" I demanded. "Did someone hurt you?" Earth might be the most dangerous one in the family, but I was no saint, and I had no problem taking down anyone who hurt my girl.

"Nothing happened. I just missed you."

Oddly, that did not make me feel better. "Something is wrong. Tell me."

Pulling back, she smiled up at me. "Nothing is wrong. My meeting didn't take as long as I expected, and I'm so happy to be home. With you."

I made a sound, still suspicious.

"Did you already go get the tree? Or should we go now?"

Did she not realize she was gone all morning? "It's in the living room."

"Oh! I can't wait to see it," she said, rushing off. "It's beautiful!" she exclaimed when I came into the room behind her. "Did you put the lights on?"

I nodded. "It's not as big as all the other ones in the house."

"Well, that hardly matters. It's the most special because you and Fletcher picked it out."

Most people would never know how sentimental Ivory was at her core.

"Earth helped too."

Her eyes widened. "Earth helped pick a tree?"

I chuckled. "He even got one for the bar."

She laughed. "Fletcher can be very convincing."

"I think we have time to decorate it before we meet Ethan and Fletcher at Rockefeller Center."

"Rockefeller Center?" she echoed. "What are we doing there?"

"Ice skating."

She gasped as though I'd told her we were flying to the moon. "Ice skating!"

I nodded. "Fletcher hasn't been."

"I can't go ice skating."

My eyes narrowed. "Why?"

She was silent for a beat. Then her chin lifted. "I don't want to."

What? "You love ice skating."

"It's too cold out," she countered.

I countered back, "That's what coats are for."

"I'm too clumsy!"

I grunted. "That never stopped you before."

Genuine dismay transformed her face, and the unmistakable glint of fear darkened her eyes.

Worry cut through me again. "Princess."

She pressed a hand to her middle. "Please, Neo. Call Ethan and tell him we can't make it."

"What's going on?" I demanded.

"Please," she whispered, face paling.

Cursing beneath my breath, I grabbed my phone and dialed Ethan. He answered on the second ring. "Neo?"

"We aren't going to be able to make it tonight," I said without preamble.

"Is everything okay?" he asked, concerned.

"Yeah, it's just been a long day. Let's meet up tomorrow."

"No skating," Ivory hurried to say.

"I thought she loved skating," Ethan murmured, clearly hearing her.

I didn't say anything because I thought she did too.

"Tomorrow is fine. How about we meet at Bryant Park at the Christmas market? I planned to take Fletch anyway."

I looked up at Ivory. "The Christmas market at Bryant Park tomorrow night?"

Relief filled her face, and she nodded eagerly. "That sounds wonderful! I can do some shopping while we're there."

"Great," I muttered. "She's going to make us carry all her bags," I warned Ethan, who just laughed and said, "I'll be ready."

Once the call was ended, I tossed the phone onto the couch. "Okay?"

She nodded, practically rushing out of the room. "I'm just going to go get changed."

"Ivory."

Her escape halted, shoulders stiffening.

"What's going on?"

"What do you mean?" she asked, voice falsely bright.

"Something is wrong, and I want to know what it is."

"Why would you think something is wrong?"

Frustrated, I stalked to where she was, taking her by the shoulders and making her face me. "You've been acting strange all day. And now you don't want to go ice skating? You are not leaving this room until you tell me what's going on."

"I'm pregnant!" The words burst out of her like an erupting volcano. The second they did, she put a hand up to her rose-red lips.

My arms dropped to my sides. I stared down at her dumbly, suddenly feeling like I was underwater and everything around me was muted. "What did you just say?"

"I didn't mean to just blurt it out like that. I wanted—"

"What did you say?"

"I'm pregnant."

A whooshing sound filled my ears. *Pregnant. Ivory is pregnant.* I looked down at her stomach, staring intently as if I would be able to see the baby inside.

Baby. Ivory is carrying my baby.

"H-how did this happen?" My voice was hoarse, even to my ears.

"I lied!" she exclaimed, tears filling her eyes.

Shocked and slightly confused, my eyes snapped up.

Without thinking, I grabbed her arms. "What do you mean you lied? Are you pregnant or not?"

"I didn't go to work this morning," she wailed. "My meeting wasn't a meeting at all. It was a doctor's appointment. And I forgot about our plans today because when I realized I might be pregnant, I couldn't even think about anything else."

"Why didn't you say anything?" I demanded.

"Because I wanted to be sure first. I didn't even think it could be possible. I was on the pill!"

My head was swimming, a thousand thoughts and emotions all firing at once. "And now you're sure?"

She nodded. "Dr. Selca ran the test twice. I'm definitely pregnant."

My eyes flew up. "That's why you were dizzy this morning?"

She nodded. "And why I can't go ice skating. What if I fall?" She pressed her hand to her stomach protectively.

All the base instincts inside me flared to life. The hot rush of possessiveness overcame everything else. If I'd felt the need to protect earlier, it was ten times greater now.

"You need to sit down," I said, scooping her up immediately, carrying her to the couch, and sitting down with her in my arms. Pulling off the stupid white heels and throwing them over the back of the couch, I said, "You can't wear these anymore. They're dangerous."

"Heels are not dangerous!"

I glowered. "They are when you wear them."

"Don't be ridiculous."

"It's not ridiculous to want you and my baby to be safe."

She fell oddly quiet, teeth sinking into her lower lip. I

know I said she was too noisy, but I preferred that over the silence.

In a soft, cajoling voice, I asked, "Sweetheart, are you mad about your shoes?"

"I thought you were going to be mad," she wailed, bursting into fresh tears.

I blinked. "Mad? Why would I be mad at you, sweetheart?"

"Because we haven't even talked about having kids. Because I'm supposed to be on the pill."

I shrugged. "You're just too pretty, sweetheart. I can't keep my hands off of you. No pill can fight that."

Her eyelashes were damp, blue eyes wide when they found mine. "Are you happy?"

Tenderness bloomed in my chest. Brushing a tear from her cheek, I whispered, "Did you really think I wouldn't be?"

Biting into her lower lip again, she shrugged. "Honestly? I wasn't sure. When we first fell in love, you ran off because you were afraid. I know you came back." She paused to smile at me and melt my pounding heart. "But a baby is a lot, and after everything you went through in the past... I guess I worried you might not be as happy as me."

"You're happy?"

"Oh my God, Neo, yes! Even when I first thought it was a possibility, I told myself not to get my hopes up. But I couldn't help it. I did. I've always longed for the big family I never had, which I found with you and the misfits, but this... this is... I am so happy. I love this baby so very much."

My heart swelled. Seeing the way her eyes glowed just talking about our child made me satisfied deep in my bones. My kid was lucky to have her. And so was I.

"I said it before, but I don't mind saying it again." She looked up. "I love you more than I'm afraid. And I admit I'm shocked, but I'm happy too."

"Really?"

Reaching down, I caressed her stomach, letting my palm settle over our child. "Yes, sweetheart. So happy." A few new tears slipped over her cheeks, and I kissed them away. "I'm not going anywhere." I promised. "Not ever."

Ivory's entire body relaxed into mine, her head nestled on my shoulder. I smiled, resting my chin on the top of her head, staring at the glowing tree.

"Tell me everything the doctor said," I prompted, rubbing her stomach. I couldn't wait until it was round with our child.

"Not much." She seemed disappointed. "He didn't even let me have a picture."

I stiffened. "What the hell kind of doctor is he?" I demanded.

"And he thinks I'm dramatic!" she exclaimed.

Who's gonna tell her?

You won't?

Fine. I will. "Well, sweetheart, you are."

Completely offended, she gasped. "Honestly, Neo! You're just as bad as he is. How do you expect me to react to the news of a baby?"

I made some soothing sounds, pushing her back against me. "It's completely reasonable to be excited."

"Of course it is," she announced. "I was worried."

A choked sound ripped from her when I peeled her away from my chest to pin her with an assessing stare. "Worried? Is something wrong? First, no picture, and then he lets you come home like that!" I fumed. Holding her gently, I got up, ready to stalk down to the place and introduce him to my fist.

Maybe I'd call Earth and have him meet me there.

"What kind of doctor lets a pregnant woman worry?" I roared.

"Neo, good heavens!" she exclaimed, patting me on the chest. "Everything is fine."

I stopped on the way to the door to look at her skeptically. "Explain."

"I worried because I was still taking my birth control, but he said it's nothing to worry about. And I made an appointment for next week. He said we can hear the heartbeat."

I felt my eyes widen. "Already?"

She nodded.

"So everything is okay?"

She nodded again.

"Fine. But if he upsets you again, he's fired."

She made some sounds and ran her hands through my hair.

I lifted a brow. "Are you placating me right now?"

"Is it working?"

"No."

"You're much better at lying than me."

I laughed.

"I'm so glad you're happy," she confided, snuggling into my chest.

"Don't ever be afraid to tell me anything, okay, princess?"

I felt her nod against me.

Awe still coursed through me, shock making me slightly lightheaded. But I really was happy. I hoped wherever my parents were, they were happy too.

"Looks like you can cross one person off your shopping list for Christmas," I said, returning to the couch.

"Who?"

"Me," I answered. "Nothing you could ever buy would be as good as this."

She giggled. "Our little Christmas surprise."

Normally, I was not a guy who liked surprises, but this one... I loved.

13

IVORY

THE SKY WAS DARK, CREATING AN OPAQUE, INKY BACKDROP for the glittering city beyond the windows. As happy as I was, the day had been stressful, and a long, relaxing soak in the bath was just what I needed.

I thought Neo would join me, but I remained in the bathtub alone. After brushing out my hair and wrapping myself up in one of Neo's red plaid flannels (rather holiday-like, wouldn't you agree?), I slipped my feet into some Versace slippers and went in search of him.

He hadn't let me out of his sight at all this afternoon, so having him be so quiet now was a little startling.

What if he changed his mind about the baby? What if, now that the news had time to sink in, he decided he wasn't as happy as he thought?

"Get a hold of yourself, Ivory," I muttered, stepping out of the bedroom.

The second I crossed the foyer, the scent of

cinnamon candles wrapped around me as well as the distinct scent of popcorn.

Intrigued, my steps quickened as I followed my nose to the living room.

Just inside the room, I stopped, lips parting in surprise.

"You like?" Neo asked, the glow of the Christmas tree at his back.

"You did this?" I whispered, gazing around at the living room.

His smile was as charming as his words. "Depends on if you like it or not."

"I don't like it," I announced.

"Well then, someone better call security 'cause someone broke in here!"

I giggled. "I love it."

He turned a little shy. "Yeah?"

I moved farther into the room, my heart turning over. The entire room was lit only by the lights on the tree and the candles near the fireplace. He'd pushed the furniture back a little to make a lot of floor space for a giant faux-fur blanket and several feather-filled holiday pillows. There was another throw blanket lying near it all, and in the center was the biggest bowl of popcorn I'd ever seen.

"Are you hungry?" I asked, giggling.

"You're eating for two now," he quipped, giving me a wink.

My stomach fluttered.

Near the bowl was a tray filled with other snacks and mugs with hot chocolate and marshmallows. "You might not like carbs," Neo said, seeing me eyeing it all. "But he does, and you can't be depriving my kid of hot chocolate at Christmas."

My hand went to my belly. "You think it's a boy?"

He shrugged. "I don't really care either way."

In front of the blanket, over by the tree, Neo set up a big screen, and across the room, a projector was aimed right at it. The screen was paused on the beginning of the movie *Home Alone*.

Behind the tree and movie screen, the large windows offered an incredible city view. But how could I look outside when literally all my dreams were in here with me?

"You made us a Christmas date?" I whispered, feeling the rush of tears behind my eyes.

"You had a stressful day, and then we had to cancel our plans with Fletcher and Ethan. Figured this might be kinda fun."

"This is everything," I said, swiping at a falling tear.

A strangled sound left his lips, and he came forward, wrapping his plaid-covered arms around me.

"Hey, we match," I observed.

"No, sweetheart. *You* are everything. You and my baby."

More tears dripped over my cheeks. "I can't seem to stop crying," I confessed. "Must be the hormones."

Dropping to his knees, Neo palmed my waist and leaned in. "Listen here, littlest misfit, go easy on your mom. Your dad loves her a whole lot."

"That's not going to get me to stop crying," I wailed.

Neo chuckled, then leaned in to gently kiss my stomach.

When he stood, he lifted me, my legs automatically winding around his waist. We kissed in the glow of the Christmas lights, a soft blanket underfoot while Neo's steady arms held me tight. His tongue was gentle and cajoling, telling me without words he loved me.

When he lifted his head, I was breathless.

"Later." He promised, kissing me one last time. "But first, we have a private show to attend."

We settled onto the blanket in our matching shirts, and Neo covered my legs with the spare blanket.

Just before he started up the movie, I called his name.

"Yes, princess?"

Without thinking, I touched my belly, smiling softly. "We should make this a tradition. Every Christmas from here on out. Just us this year, but next year, we'll make it for three."

In the soft glow of the room, he smiled. "Yeah, I like that."

And just like that, our Christmas date grew into something even more special, a lifelong Christmas tradition.

14

ETHAN

THE BLOWING WIND WAS CRISP, THE SCENT OF SNOW HEAVY in the air, promising more than just the fluttering flakes we were enjoying now.

It was dark, but there were so many lights the streets glowed.

"Are we almost there?" Fletcher was impatient against my ear.

Pausing to hike his slipping body higher on my back, I said, "Almost."

"Just tell me already!" he implored, releasing the grip he had around my neck.

"Don't even think about it," I told him.

He made a rude sound, but his arms looped around me once again.

"This is ridiculous," he grumbled.

"You love it," I teased.

"Me?" He scoffed.

"You mean being given a piggyback ride through the streets of New York City while being blindfolded is not something you love?" I stopped walking. "My apologies. I'll just turn around and go home, then. You can remove that blindfold."

I started lowering him to the ground.

"Wait!"

I paused, grateful he couldn't see my wide smile. "Change your mind?"

"Keep going."

Adjusting him again, I started off.

Up ahead, Rockefeller Center sat like the centerpiece it was. The seventy-nine-foot giant tree was lit with thousands of colorful lights, and the glowing star on its top was a pride of the city. It towered grandly over The Rink, a famous ice skating rink, which glowed from purple LED lights and was surrounded by well over one hundred flags furiously flying in the wind.

Slowing my footsteps, I came to a stop, enjoying the feel of Fletcher against my back, legs wrapped around me and impatient breathing at my neck.

In my quest to give Fletch a memorable Christmas, I'd also given one to myself.

"E…" Fletcher worried. "I said keep going. I'm not embarrassed."

I laughed beneath my breath. "Why on earth would you be embarrassed?"

"Because I'm a grown man getting a piggyback ride through the city."

"Down you go," I said, lowering so he could stand.

"No!" He clung tighter, refusing to put his feet down. It was a good thing I did so many squats at the gym. "I said I want to see my surprise."

"We're here."

He paused. Then, "Oh."

When he was standing, I turned, smiling at how he was turning his head like he was gazing around even though he still had on a blindfold. "How's the view?"

His lower lip jutted out in a pout. "Not funny."

Unable to deny myself, I leaned in, claiming his lips. He jolted in surprise at first but recovered quickly to moan lightly in his throat and grab the front of my jacket.

His nose was cold, as were his lips, but as I rubbed against him, his skin began to warm. Our tongues swirled lazily, a bit of the crisp wind slipping into my mouth. Forgetting where I was and thinking only about the man in my arms, I pulled him flush against me, earning another little groan. Swallowing it down, I tilted my head and kissed deeper.

His hand released my coat to pat gently against my chest, reminding me we were on the street. As I drew back, I kissed the end of his nose, and he smiled, shy.

"Maybe we should save this blindfold for later," he whispered.

I caught his hand. "Come on. Let's just go home now."

He laughed. "Ethan!"

"Fine." I agreed. "Close your eyes."

"They're already covered!"

"So I can take off the cover." I remained patient. I loved the way his feet danced a bit over the pavement, his excitement showing.

"They're closed."

"Be a good boy and don't look," I said, removing the covering, tucking it into my pocket for later.

His eyes were definitely closed, and as I stared, a wayward snowflake caught on his lashes, which were fanned over his cheek.

"Ready?" I asked, throat clogged with love.

"Duh!"

"All right, open."

He wasn't slow or deliberate. Instead, his lids popped open like a can of processed biscuits.

"Rockefeller Center!" he exclaimed as if it were his first time seeing it even though we'd been here not long ago for the tree lighting. "I love it here!"

"I know." I found it completely charming he thought this was the surprise and was so happy with it. It seemed it wouldn't matter where I took Fletcher, somewhere new or somewhere we'd been a thousand times. He would still be grateful.

"Do you know why I brought you here?" I asked.

"To see the lights?"

I nodded. "But there's more."

"What?"

Taking his hand, I led him closer toward the lit-up rink. "Thought you might like the try ice skating."

"Really?"

I nodded.

He glanced at the rink, and his face fell. "Looks like they're closed already. Look, it's empty."

"They aren't closed. They're waiting for us."

His eyes rounded. "You rented out the ice skating rink at Rockefeller Center?"

"For a little while."

He threw himself at me. Something I was very used to and very in love with. I caught him easily, steadying our weight. "Thank you!" He drew back. "We could have just come to skate with everyone else,"

"I don't want everyone else. Just you," I told him.

He smiled, clearly pleased.

"And since Ivory and Neo can't make it, it truly is just us."

"Ivory and Neo were supposed to come?" He perked up. "That must be what Neo meant when he said I would see Ivory later."

I nodded. "Yes, but I think she had a long day, so they send their regrets."

"It's okay. I like being alone with you."

I leaned forward to steal another kiss, but he grabbed my hand. "Come on! Let's go!"

Ah, denied a kiss. But thankfully, the sound of his happy laughter was a close second.

15

FLETCHER

I STARED DOWN AT THE HEAVY SKATES CLUTCHED IN MY hands, and I realized something. Something pretty important.

"Ethan?"

"What, puppy?" he asked, already on the closest bench, removing his shoes.

"I don't know how to ice-skate."

A soft noise left his throat, and a little part of me felt comforted. Ethan's soft noises always made me feel like that. Just having him beside me was a comfort.

I loved him. So much. The amount of thought he'd put into everything this season made my heart swell every time I just looked at him.

"Are you nervous?" he asked, abandoning his skates to come over to me.

"Maybe a little," I admitted.

"I've skated before, so I'll show you how. It's pretty easy. You'll get the hang of it in no time."

"What if I fall?"

He leaned in beside my ear. "Then I'll kiss any scrapes you get."

Oh, suddenly, the idea of falling appealed more to me than staying on my feet.

"Keep looking at me like that, and the ice is going to melt," he murmured, still at my ear.

Despite the cold, my cheeks heated.

"Come on. I'll help you," he said, leading me over to the bench.

Once we both had our skates on, Ethan stood, moving as graceful as ever.

"Maybe I should start working out," I muttered, wobbling even as I tried to stand.

"You can if you want. But I love you the way you are."

"Don't let go," I said, gripping his hand for dear life.

"Never," he said as we moved toward the pristine ice.

It was so beautiful and untouched. It glistened and was so smooth to the touch it almost appeared to be glass. The lights around the rink glowed purple, and rising over it was the giant tree. Flags whipped and flapped above us, and more string lights were hung around the buildings nearby.

"It's sort of like roller-blading," Ethan said, transferring my hands to the railing so he could step onto the ice. "Have you ever done that?"

I frowned. "No."

He made that soft sound again. "Well, now I know what we can do at the beach this summer."

"We're going to the beach?"

"Do you want to?"

"Yes!" I exclaimed, forgetting I was on skates and

letting go of the railing. I started to topple, but Ethan caught me around the waist.

"Maybe we should talk about the beach later," he mused. "Come on, then," he said, drawing me onto the ice.

"Wait! I don't know how."

"I'll hold your hand."

I went because, really, I'd go anywhere he asked me to. My legs shook like I was just learning how to walk as I stepped onto the thick ice. Ethan held both my hands and started skating backward, towing me slowly along.

"Hey, you're really good!"

He smiled. "I've had some practice."

I rolled my eyes. "Is there anything you aren't good at?"

"Making cookies," he deadpanned.

I laughed because he was right.

"Push off a little, like this," he instructed, showing me how to move.

I tried it out, pushing forward. We glided over the ice, the wind nipping at my cheeks. I was still wobbly, and he still held my hand, but I was upright.

My laugh bounced off the retaining walls around us, echoing up toward the tree. "I'm doing it!"

We stayed like that for a while, going around the small rink, Ethan holding my hands and skating backward, guiding me.

I liked the sound the skates made cutting over the ice. I liked when Ethan dug his blades in, making a cutting sound to push off. The wind made my cheeks sting and my lips were dry, but I couldn't stop smiling.

"I want to do it on my own now," I announced.

Worry crossed Ethan's features, but he nodded. "All

right," he said, slowing down and moving up beside me. "Stay close to the side in case you need to grab the rail."

I nodded and then pushed off, wobbled and tilted at first, but I threw my arms out for balance. When I was halfway around the rink, I finally took my eyes off the ice in front of me to flash a smile. "Look! I'm doing it."

"I'm so impressed. You're doing much better than I did my first time on the ice."

Encouraged, I pushed forward a little more. We skated for a while, Ethan staying close, always there in case I fell. By the third lap around, I was feeling more confident, so I pushed away from the railing toward the center of the rink.

My scarf blew back over my shoulder, and I gazed up toward the sky to smile.

The toe of my skate caught in the ice. I jolted and then pitched backward, arms flailing.

Oomph. Instead of hitting the ice, my back hit something much softer, and very familiar arms went around me from behind.

Thump. We both landed in a heap on the ice with me right on top of Ethan, him breaking my fall. Rolling off him, I freaked out. "Ethan! Are you okay?"

He was sprawled out on the ice, flat on his back.

"Ethan!"

"Fletch," he moaned.

Worry made me panic, and I draped myself partly over his chest. "Ethan, are you hurt? Should I call for help?"

Grabbing my scarf, he pulled me in, his lips moving. I leaned down, straining to hear what he might say.

"Need mouth-to-mouth."

It took a moment to register. When it did, I scowled. "E! I thought I hurt you!"

He laughed. It was such a happy sound that I laughed too.

"You jerk," I muttered around a laugh.

"Aw, puppy, don't be mad."

"Are you really okay? You aren't hurt?"

"I'm fine," he said, not making any moves to get up. "Are you okay?"

I nodded. "Guess I got too confident."

"You did well, my good boy." He promised, then shifted his stare upward. "Look at that view," he murmured.

Since he was still lying flat on the ice, I lay down beside him, following his gaze.

"It's the biggest Christmas tree I've ever seen," I said, gazing at the Rockefeller tree rising above us.

"It's quite impressive."

"I still like our tree best," I said, thinking of the small, kind of crooked thing. We filled it in with lots of ornaments, and we even used some of those rock-hard cookies we tried to make. They were terrible to eat, but they made pretty good ornaments. We also used some tinsel. I'd never look at tinsel the same way ever again.

"Me too," he said fondly, finding my hand and bringing it to his lips to kiss it. I frowned because there was a glove between us. I started to pull it off, but Ethan stopped me.

"What are you doing?"

"I can't feel your lips."

His eyes warmed, but he shook his head. "Your fingers will freeze."

I made a face.

In a swift movement, Ethan jolted up, grabbing me at the waist and toppling us back over so I was lying along his chest and our skates were tangled together.

"What are you doing?" I was breathless.

"I thought you wanted to feel my lips."

I glanced around. But since he rented the place out, we were the only ones here. Smiling, I puckered my lips.

"My little kiss monster." His voice was affectionate and made me feel loved. Everything he did made me feel loved.

"Ethan?" I interrupted him before he could kiss me.

"Hm?"

"This really is the best Christmas ever."

The joy in his eyes made my heart beat unevenly, and for the first time in my whole life, I thought maybe all the stuff I missed in the past was okay because now I could experience it all for the first time with him.

"I love you," he whispered, then covered my mouth with his.

Everything around us was icy and cold, but for once, I didn't mind the cold. I didn't even feel any of it because Ethan kept me warm.

16

"We're going out."

I turned from the windows overlooking the street in Brooklyn that I'd come to know as home. "What?"

"Brooklyn has some gorgeous light displays this time of year. We're going for a walk to look at them all."

"I don't want to."

Emogen rolled her eyes. "Is that why I keep catching you staring out the window, trying to see them all?"

"I'm admiring the new windows I had put in."

She made a sound. "They're nice, but they aren't *that* nice."

I remained silent. I wasn't going out. My appearance would just distract from all the lights anyway. We wouldn't be spectators out for a holiday walk. We'd turn into the attraction.

I wasn't as insecure as I used to be. I'd been modeling for Ivory's line, given a few interviews, and even started back to work. I could take the lingering glances, the curiosity, and even the fear. But sometimes I just didn't feel like it.

I didn't want Christmas to somehow be tarnished with my face.

"Get your coat," Em said, ignoring my stubborn silence.

"I'm not going."

"Then I guess you won't need this," she mused, producing a small box from behind her back. It was wrapped in plaid paper and had a big red bow.

Instant curiosity drew me closer. "What is that?"

"Well, it's a gift for you. But since you aren't coming…"

I snatched it from her hand, holding it between us. "This is for me?"

"Who else would it be for?"

I expected a sassy retort to roll off her tongue. I did not expect the whispered tone and soft eyes.

I hugged the box against my chest, crushing the bow under my hold. "But it's not even Christmas yet."

"Like I said, I thought you would need it. But since you aren't going…" She reached for the present, and I growled. "You don't scare me, Ander Todd," she intoned, not even hesitating a little.

"Mine!" I told her, jerking away, still hugging it tight.

Her hands went to her hips. "You act like you've never had a Christmas present before."

"Not from you," I said, gazing down at it. It's true I was no stranger to gifts, but this one seemed more personal. This one was not an obligation. This one was wanted.

"Well, damn," she said softly. "Now I'm nervous. It's not anything special."

"It is," I replied, carrying it with me to sit on the couch. "'Cause it's from you."

Spreading my knees, I pulled the coffee table close, patting it so she would come sit. She did, maneuvering so she was right between my knees.

I stared at the gift for a while, simply taking in the red and black plaid paper and the velvety red bow. It didn't even matter what was inside.

"Open it." She beckoned, a little nervousness in her tone.

I leaned forward over the box and into her personal space to kiss her. "Thank you," I whispered against her lips, then kissed her once more.

"Maybe you should look at it before you thank me."

I shook my head even as I tugged the end of the bow. "I don't need to."

"Well, I could definitely use more practice."

Intrigued, I ripped the paper off, tossing it onto the floor. Without hesitation, I pulled the top off the box and shoved aside the red tissue paper.

My hand closed around the thick, soft material. It was so soft I rubbed the pads of my fingers against it again. Lifting the cobalt-blue yarn out of the box, I glanced up. "A hat?"

Her smile turned into a slight grimace. "Like I said, I could use more practice."

Realization dawned, and I looked to the basket of yarn she kept near the sofa. My stare flew back to her. "You made this?" I asked, awed.

"My mama taught me how to crochet. She told me that gifts made by the hands and heart were best."

I stared down at the blue fabric, my vision going a little blurry. My chest was tight and my lungs squeezed, but it really wasn't uncomfortable.

I didn't realize I was squeezing the material so tight until Emogen's hand slid over one of mine. "Hey."

Embarrassingly, a choked sound ripped from my throat. Keeping my stare trained on the knitted cap and our hands, I said, "Your mama was right."

Emotion pummeled me, and because it was so unexpected, it pummeled me again. One moment, I'd been staring out into the street, gazing at the lights strung in the trees, and feeling a melancholy sort of way, and the next... the next, my hands were filled with something made, not bought. Something the woman I loved above everything else worked over, spent hours using her hands to craft... She didn't spend a cent, yet it was made with something far more valuable.

Her love.

"*Em.*" The word was not spoken; it was felt.

Her soft humming sound was so familiar to me and so comforting that my vision went watery all over again.

"If you don't like it, just say so. You don't have to cry."

She was teasing. Trying to lighten the emotions rolling off me in waves. She knew this would mortify me... but why should it?

I'd spent a lot of time feeling nothing but pain and anger. Why should I be embarrassed about feeling something far better?

This is why I didn't just die. A stray thought, but no less poignant because it seemed so random. But was it really? I wondered many times after waking up from the fire why I hadn't just died. I'd even thought that death would have been far kinder.

But now I knew.

I didn't die because I had life waiting on the other side. Not just any life, though. Love.

"Let me see you." Emogen beckoned, those four words a love language all their own.

I lifted my chin immediately, letting her see the unshed tears and the emotion nearly taking me to my knees.

"I really love it," I whispered.

"I know you do." Her voice was thick too, and I was glad to know I wasn't the only one affected.

The pads of her thumbs swept under my eyes as if she would catch all the tears I hadn't let fall. No longer did I wince when she touched my scars. She did it so often I barely noticed anymore.

She acted like she didn't even see the horrible disfigurement that made me look like a two-faced man. One side handsome, the other a beast. She loved them both equally. Her attention never favored one over the other.

It took her a second to get me to relent the tight hold I had on the hat, but when I finally did, she lifted it, and I bent my head.

My hair was growing back, and it was finally gaining some length. But the growth pattern on the left side was a little skewed. In plain talk, the scarring made it look like I had a million cowlicks, and the hair stuck out at all different angles. Styling helped some, but usually, the wildness could not be contained.

I hated it, of course, but Em told me to be grateful I had hair.

I settled into a disgruntled sort of acceptance, and I favored a lot of hats. A patch of skin was still bald near my ear, and I was starting to think perhaps that hair would never grow back at all.

"I tried to make it a little bigger so it would be kinda slouchy. But I'm no Givenchy, so we'll just have to make allowances," she said, carefully pulling the thick, soft fabric over my head.

I caught her wrist, tugging one of her hands down to kiss the center of her palm. "Givenchy who? You're my favorite designer now."

She giggled. "There you go with that charm, Ander Todd."

I smiled.

Going back to what she was doing, Em pulled it down, adjusting the fabric. "It will cover your ears too. Keep them warm."

And offer me some protection from prying eyes. She didn't say that part out loud. She didn't need to. I knew.

Pulling back, she looked at her handiwork. A little pride lit those chestnut eyes, and my heart warmed. "It fits!"

"Hey," I said, drawing her back in, taking her hands in mine. "You made this for me."

"Thought you could wear it when you took me walking to see the lights."

"I'll wear it every day."

"Is that a yes?" Her eyes were hopeful.

As if I could say no.

"Get your coat," I told her, kissing the end of her nose.

When she came back, she was wearing hers along with a large green, red, and white plaid scarf draped around her neck and shoulders. Instead of a hat, she had on a pair of furry white earmuffs.

My heart turned over.

Despite my reservations about going out, I slid into my coat. It didn't matter if people looked at me tonight because I wouldn't notice. I would be busy looking at my girl.

"Don't you want to look at your hat before you go?" she asked, pausing in the doorway.

Catching her around the waist, I pulled her out onto the front stoop, shutting the door behind us. The garland she'd insisted I hang around the arched door glowed with white lights, making this concrete slab seem more welcoming than before.

The wreath on the front door probably weighed ten pounds and was lit too. The rug underfoot was red and green striped.

"I don't need to see it. I can feel it. I love it. And I love you, sweetheart."

She smiled, ducking into my chest.

"Hey." I tapped her on the shoulder.

When she lifted her head, I pointed up. Her laughter seemed to drift off with the snow dancing in the winter wind. "When did you do that?" she exclaimed, staring up at the giant ball of mistletoe hanging overhead.

I shrugged, tugging her body closer against mine. "Maybe it was Santa."

Her eyes twinkled. "Maybe I should kiss him instead."

I growled. "You know what I do to people that touch you, sweetheart. Do you really want to deprive all these kids of Santa?"

Laughing lightly, she tugged the rim of my hat, and I dipped close to kiss her. Wintry air slipped between our parted lips, mingling with the heat of our breath and twisting around our tongues. The hot-and-cold sensation was thrilling, almost like breathing in after eating a candy cane.

Em sighed into my mouth, and I lifted so her boots dangled over the ground and our mouths fused so tight I didn't even have to share her with the air.

Mine.

Gently setting her back on her feet, I threaded our gloved fingers together. "C'mon then. Let's go see the lights."

"You want to see them too," she said as we went down the concrete steps.

"Careful." I cautioned, worrying about the thin layer of newly fallen snow.

At the end of our small walkway leading to the side-walk, she stopped, lifting her face toward the sky. All the trees lining the block were lit with white lights and cast a glow down upon her upturned cheeks. Snowflakes clung to her wild curls, and she stuck her tongue out, trying to catch a few.

My heart swelled just looking at her. *It was all worth it.* Everything that led me to this moment.

"It's really beautiful," she mused a few moments later, her voice not having to compete with the usual sounds of the city. The hour was late, most traffic and noise asleep. All that remained was the crisp night air and dark sky, which acted as the perfect backdrop to a city lit from within.

Other couples wandered hand in hand, also taking in the lights and the quiet, also understanding this was something special and not often found in the city.

We went hand and hand through Brooklyn, the twinkling light displays and decorated homes making me see this part of the city as I never had before. The scent of roasting chestnuts wafted close, dancing beneath my nose and making my stomach growl.

"Let's go," Em said, staring across the street to the cart.

The tip of my nose was cold, my cheeks numb, and there was a line at the chestnut cart. I caught a few lingering glances, and my automatic reaction was to duck my head.

"You want to wait over there while I get these?" she asked, stepping a little closer and gazing up.

Leaning down, I kissed her softly. "Now why would I do that when I can stand right here beside you?"

She stayed tight against my side until it was our turn to order.

"Ooh, you have cider too?"

"Yes, ma'am," the man behind the cart answered.

"Then two of those too, please," she ordered.

When I handed over the cash, I felt the man's stare, and bravely, I met it. I didn't look quite as heinous as before, with some scruff covering my lower jaw and the hat covering my ear. But even still, people noticed. People still stared.

I felt my hackles rise, and the beast I shared my body with rumbled to life. At my side, Em shifted and took a sip of her cider.

Not tonight, I thought.

"If you're wondering where I got my hat, it's limited edition," I said, smiling directly at the vendor. "My girl made it."

Surprised, the man blinked. But then he smiled. "Well, she did a fine job." When he held out my change, I waved it back. "Keep it."

His eyes widened because it was a rather large tip. "Thank you."

"Merry Christmas," Em called, tugging me away. When the stand was behind us, I felt her gaze. "You did good, boo. Real good."

Her praise made the beast in me purr like a giant cat.

We walked a little farther, turning onto a street that was so lit up our steps faltered. Holding hands, we stood and stared down the block at how the lights draped over the street and twinkled in the trees. Every rowhome was decorated and lined with garland. Snow clung to the decorations, making them even more beautiful.

"It's beautiful." Em's voice was a hushed whisper.

"Yes."

We stood in the center of the street under the glittering lights, snow fluttering around. The crinkle of the chestnut bag made me look down, and Em held the fragrant nut up to my lips.

I took it, eyes not leaving hers, and bit into it slowly.

"You know," I mused, chewing, "I always think of these when I look into your eyes."

Surprise flitted across her face. "Really?"

"Mm." I agreed. "Rich. Warm. Comforting."

"You make brown seem a lot better than I ever thought it was."

"Feed me another one," I demanded.

She made a sound and muttered, "Spoiled."

When I was chewing another one, we both gazed back out over the impressive street that nearly burst with holiday spirit.

A heavy feeling settled over me, making me shift closer to my girl.

"Ander?" she asked, sensing the change in me immediately.

I smiled, making some of the worry in her eyes evaporate.

"I wondered once if I would even be able to walk the streets this year. If I would be able to eat chestnuts and be visible. I thought my life was over."

I gazed back out at the illuminated street, throat feeling tight. *I almost missed this.*

"Your life isn't over, boo. It's just beginning."

"I didn't want to come out," I echoed, still facing the street. But suddenly, the magical street had nothing on her. Rotating, I stepped close so our bodies practically bumped. The fringe on the end of her ridiculously large scarf blew and clung to my coat, and snow still freckled her dark hair.

Her nose was cold. It shined beneath the twinkling lights.

"I came out for you. But you came out for me, didn't you?"

She smiled.

Leaning in, I pressed our foreheads together and then the tips of our icy noses. "I'm gonna keep you," I whispered.

As we kissed in the center of the street, among the lights and snow, Christmas whispered in my ear, telling me exactly what I needed to do.

17

"Pops!" I called for like the hundredth time. "Dinner!"

Any other time, he'd be hot-footing it to the table, grumbling about what took me so long to feed him.

And where the hell was Ander?

Leaving behind the newly remodeled kitchen, which was fancier than anything I'd ever seen, I wandered through the living room toward the stairs, which were wrapped with pine garland and bows.

"I'm tossing dinner in the trash!" I yelled up the stairs.

Those fools didn't even come running for that. I was getting soft, I guess. I was going to have to actually toss it in the trash at least once if I wanted them to hustle when I threatened.

Ding-dong!

Spinning from the stairs, I glanced around at the front door. We weren't expecting anyone. Of course, our family just showed up when they felt like it, so I guess it didn't matter.

"I'm answering the door!" I yelled up the stairs. *That should bring him running.*

It didn't.

Frowning, I went and pulled open the door. December wind rushed in immediately, along with some drifting snow.

"I thought I told you not to answer the door," Ander intoned, glowering from the other side.

"Ander! What are you doing out here? I thought you were *in* the house."

He leaned in and smiled. "Missing me, huh?"

The blue hat I'd knitted was pulled over his forehead, the color bringing out the blue in his eyes, exactly as I knew it would. Butterflies danced around in my stomach, but he didn't need to know it.

I scoffed. "I was about to throw your dinner in the trash."

His blue orbs twinkled. "Aw, sweetheart, but then I'll be hungry."

I made a rude noise. "What are you even doing out here?" Leaning around him, I looked onto the stoop. "Is Pops with you?"

"He had somewhere to be."

Pushing my fists against my hips, I asked, "Where could he possibly need to be at this hour?" My eyes narrowed. "Why are your hands behind your back?"

He pulled them around and, with them, a large bouquet of red roses. The long stems were tied with a large red ribbon. "Will you go on a date with me, Emogen Robinson?"

As he spoke, white puffs formed in front of him, swirling in the space between us. When I just stood and stared, he pushed the roses closer to me, their delicate petals quivering just a little in the cold.

A giddy feeling made my toes curl against the floor as I reached for the flowers. "They're very beautiful, boo. Thank you."

"Is that a yes?"

"Always." I confirmed, the scent of roses tickling my nose.

"Get your coat."

Surprise made me jolt. "You mean like now?"

He smiled. "Now's as good a time as any."

"What about dinner?"

"What about it?"

A horn from the street burst through the night, making me look up. Ander shifted so I could see the G-Wagon at the curb. "Driver's waiting," he quipped.

"I'm not dressed for a date!" I exclaimed, glancing down at my leggings and oversized sweater.

Ander's boots stepped over the threshold, his coat-covered arm snatching me around the waist to pull me into his cold form. "You don't have to worry about the way you look with me, sweetheart, because to me, you are always beautiful."

"I'll get my coat."

He gave my ass a pat. "Go on then."

I couldn't help squealing in excitement as I raced into the kitchen to turn off all the appliances and gently place the bouquet on the island.

I left dinner on the stove and the lights on the tree lit as I grabbed my coat and scarf, rushing back to the door.

"Whoa." He cautioned, catching me around the waist. More snow drifted inside around his feet, and a few fat flakes clung to the material of his hat. "Put it on before you come out."

"I'll put it on in the car," I said, trying to rush past.

Tsk-tsk. He clucked his tongue. "Now, or you'll freeze." Taking the garment, he held it out for me to stuff my arms inside. When I was done, I whirled to face him.

"Where are we going?" I asked, unable to contain my curiosity.

He chuckled, doing the buttons up. "You'll see." He practically teased, looping the scarf around my neck, giving the ends a tug so I came out onto the porch, right up against his chest.

Despite standing in the winter night, the kiss we shared was warm. It also made me buzz with anticipation.

What is he up to now?

"Ander?" I asked as we were getting into the G-Wagon.

"What, sweetheart?"

"Is Pops okay?"

"He's fine. I promise."

And just like that, the little anxiety I felt smoothed over, and I pushed my hand into his waiting one.

OUR RIDE STOPPED IN CENTRAL PARK. A VERY FAMILIAR section of the park.

"Pops?" I called, flinging open the door and nearly jumping from the back.

"Hey, girlie! I was starting to wonder if you refused to come."

Pops was dressed in his driving uniform, standing beside a large white carriage that was draped in garland and white lights. There was even a small wreath hanging on the back of the carriage.

Finnegan was standing by, ready to go with some silver bells lining his leads.

"Isn't work over for the day?" I wondered.

The familiar feel of Ander's palm slid over the small of my back, and I leaned into the touch naturally.

"I had a special client reserve a special time," Pops replied.

Tipping my chin up, I asked Ander, "You did this?"

"Wanted to go on a Christmas carriage ride with my favorite girl."

"Can we do that?" I asked, gazing out over the park. It wasn't as dark as it usually was because of the holiday lights wrapped around the trees. But still… "Carriages aren't running at this hour."

He pecked a kiss to my nose. "Did you forget who I am?"

Ah, yes. Mr. Big Head himself. Ander Todd, owner of Todd House and the carriages that ran through the park. "I didn't forget," I whispered, curling my hands into the lapels of his coat. "I just don't care."

He smiled, the corners of his eyes crinkling a bit. "I know, and I love you for it. But sometimes a man has to use his connections to spoil his girl." After a quick kiss, he nudged me toward the carriage. "Come on. Up you go."

Pops went into formal driver mode, bowing a little before pulling open the door. Ander helped me up into the deep green interior of the carriage before climbing in next to me. The seats were piled high with blankets, and on the seat across from us was a tray with two cups of hot chocolate, the Kismet label on the front.

"Warm enough?" Ander asked once we were covered and holding the drinks.

I nodded, snuggling into the seat and gazing across

the expansive park. It was a winter wonderland in the center of a hectic city. "I haven't been on a carriage ride since I was a little girl."

He made a noise. "How can that be? Pops drives them daily."

"It's his work, and these rides are expensive. You charge too much." I informed him.

His laughter was punctuated by more white puffs of breath bursting around his head. Tucking his arm around me, his nose nudged my cheek. "Well, it's time you had another, and tonight is free," he said, kissing the top of my head.

Sighing, I leaned my cheek against his shoulder as the carriage started moving. The air was cold, making my cheeks prickle and my nose turn numb. The sounds of Finnegan clip-clopping over the pavement made a soothing cadence, and the slight jostling of the old wooden carriage gave me an excuse to push farther into Ander's side.

The silver jingle bells attached to Finnegan's reins and harness filled the park with a light, jolly sound as we passed under trees draped with lights. The freshly fallen snow glowed under the twinkling lights and draped over branches and statues. Rising around the park, tall city buildings created a magical skyline and had a way of making a girl feel small.

The ice skating rink was lit up, tall golden trees illuminating its edges, but the ice was empty. In fact, no one was out here at all. It was as if we had Central Park all to ourselves.

"It's so beautiful," I murmured, lifting my face and breathing in deeply. The air was so fresh and crisp I felt it all the way in the back of my throat.

"You know I've never done this at Christmas," he

mused, gazing out across the vacant park. "It really is beautiful. I can see why it's such a tourist attraction."

"You?" I said incredulous, lifting my head to look at him. "Mr. Society himself?"

He made a low noise. Kind of a laugh, kind of a groan. "Guess I was waiting for you."

Leaning up, I pecked a kiss against his lips before looking out over the park once more.

"Your lips are cold," he whispered against my ear. "Drink this." He reminded me, tapping on the cup my hands wrapped around.

Warm, thick chocolate enveloped my tongue, sliding easily down my throat. I felt its warmth coat my belly and sighed happily.

When the carriage drove over a small stone bridge, a new sound mingled with the jingling bells and clopping of Finnegan's hooves.

Tilting my head, I listened to the faint sound as it grew louder.

"Is that music?" I murmured, straightening up to look around with sharp eyes. The lustrous, flutelike chords danced in the air, flirting with the fat snowflakes fluttering down from a dark sky.

"Is that a violin?" I wondered. Gasping, I turned wide eyes to Ander. "Is that Fletcher?"

His lips curled upward. "Fletcher will be happy to know you recognize his playing."

Grabbing his arm, I gave it a little squeeze. "What's Fletcher doing out here?"

His eyes were like a caress. "I asked him to come."

He was playing a classic Christmas song. Every chord filled the air despite him being somewhere I couldn't see him. He played so passionately, so wholeheartedly, I swear it seemed even the snowflakes fell a little more gracefully so as not to disturb the song.

"But why?" I finally echoed.

Straightening off the bench, Ander shifted toward me, the blanket we shared falling into our laps. His gloved hand cupped the back of my head, and the softness in his stare made everything else fall away.

"For you," he whispered. His attention drifted over my shoulder, his eyes seeming to settle upon something nearby. "For this."

Following his gaze, I twisted around and gasped.

"Is that...?" My voice fell away. "Is that for us?"

His cheek brushed against my hair when he leaned over my shoulder. "Who else would it be for?"

Another breathless sort of sound erupted from my throat as the carriage slowly rolled to a stop. Hands gripping the top of the carriage, I leaned out just a little to stare at his surprise. In the center of the clearing, a giant clear globe sat in the snow. The giant bubble was strung with white lights and hanging from the center of the ceiling was what looked like a freaking chandelier. Beneath it was a table draped in white, and I could see the flickering of candles.

"Ander," I whispered.

"I know you made dinner earlier, but I made it too," he explained.

Spinning, I was surprised to see him standing outside the carriage in the open door. I hadn't even heard him move.

I didn't know what to say, what to do. No one had ever done anything even close to this for me before. It was like something in the books I read. But it wasn't a story; it was real, and he was standing there underneath glowing lights in a giant park he seemed to commandeer as beautiful music floated through the chilly air.

"Well, go on then, girlie. Don't make him wait," Pops called from his driver's seat.

Startled, I glanced over. I'd forgotten he was here.

"You knew about this?" I asked, fingering the thick scarf around my neck.

"I gave my blessing."

My brow wrinkled.

"Em." Ander beckoned, and then I was moving, allowing him to lift me down out of the carriage and take my hand.

"It looks like a big snow globe," I said as we approached, our boots crunching over the snow.

"It does." He agreed, but I kept the snow on the outside. "Didn't want to freeze."

"I can't believe you did this." I was still in awe, barely able to even digest something so incredible.

The music was louder now that we neared the clear dome. "Where's Fletch?" I glanced around.

"It's just us tonight," he said, tugging me into his side.

"It's even more impressive up close," I murmured, taking in the clear dome twinkling with lights. There was a small opening on one side and, above it, a giant gold bow.

A bouquet of red roses sat in the center of the white table, small candles flickering beneath them. Rose petals covered the white fur rug on the ground. Yes. There was a white fur rug.

Ander started in first, but I grabbed his hand. "Your boots!"

"What about them?"

"You can't step in there with dirty shoes."

His eyes rolled. "It's freezing out here, sweetheart."

"Boo." I beckoned, making him growl.

I smiled when he kicked off the boots and then reached to help me with mine. Leaving them outside the dome, we stepped in, our sock-covered feet sinking into the softness of the rug.

"It's warmer in here," I murmured, gazing around at every detail. The candles gave off a light vanilla scent, and it mingled with fresh rose.

There was a silver tray on the table with a bottle of champagne, two crystal flutes, and two plates covered with silver domes.

"You really did make dinner?" I mused.

He grimaced. "I had someone else make it."

"And all I did was make you a hat." I scoffed, still gazing around in astonishment.

His signature growl rumbled in the small space as he caught me around the waist, towing me into the circle of his body. "This hat is the best thing anyone has ever given me. It will never be *just a hat*."

I gave the blue fabric a little tug and smiled. "Thank you, boo. Thank you for all of this."

Our lips met softly, the kiss languid and unhurried. We stood suspended in time where we truly did exist inside a snow globe, the moment forever captured.

When at last we parted, something unexpected glimmered in his sapphire eyes. Something that looked a whole lot like nerves.

"Ander?"

"This isn't everything," he said, straightening to his full height and clearing his throat. "There's more."

18

ANDER

NOT LONG AGO, MY LIFE WAS DIVIDED INTO TWO. BEFORE the fire and after. I thought my life was over. I wondered why I even survived.

Then came Em. I realized I couldn't have an after if there was never a before.

I wouldn't go back. I wouldn't trade even the darkest of nights and the hellish moments of pure pain. All of that led me to where I stood today.

All of it led me to this woman. To truths I never would have looked deep enough before to find.

I felt her stare like it was the weight of the world, and though I was suddenly intensely nervous, I was also not afraid.

Pulling out a black velvet box, I lowered slowly onto one knee.

Her light gasp made my insides flutter and my hands

unsteady as I opened the box to reveal a glimmering diamond.

Her chestnut eyes widened, and her plump lower lip quivered as she stared transfixed at the black velvet box sitting open in my grasp.

"Em, sweetheart, I meant it when I said I was keeping you. Forever. Always. 'Til the end of time. That fire was the worst thing to ever happen in my life, but it brought me the best. It brought me you. And you, baby, you taught me how to see past the surface and look at what truly matters most. You're mine. I'm keeping you. So will you, Emogen Robinson, be the beauty to my beast and keep me too?"

Tears spilled over her cheeks, a little sob vibrating her throat. "You wanna get married?"

"Was I not clear enough?" I asked, tugging the ring out of the box and tossing it over my shoulder.

"Really?" she whispered.

"Really, sweetheart." Then, a little cheeky, I asked, "Can I get up now?"

She made a sound like she was just noticing I was on one knee. Rushing forward, she pulled me to my feet.

"Well?" I demanded.

She laughed. "Yes!" Throwing her arms around my neck, she hugged me tight. "Yes, of course I'll marry you."

Satisfaction suffused me, making everything inside me warm. A growl rumbled in my chest. Clearly, the beast in me was satisfied too.

"Give me your hand," I said, already reaching for it.

I slipped the platinum diamond band onto her finger, pulling up her hand to kiss the emerald-cut diamond in the center. "Mine," I declared.

Tugging her hand free, she looked at the ring and gasped. "This is too big!"

"It's a perfect fit," I refuted. I knew it would be. I snooped in all her jewelry so I'd get the right size.

"You know what I mean," she intoned, still staring at the sparkling diamond.

Oh, I knew. The center stone was a flawless two carats. I wanted to get bigger, but I thought she'd refuse. So I settled for a smaller center stone and had the band encrusted with diamonds too. There was more than one way to get three carats of sparkle on my girl.

"You don't like the ring I picked for you?"

Finally tearing her eyes from the stone, she looked up, hearing the bit of hurt I put in the words.

A soft sound floated above us when she cupped my head. "Of course I love it, boo. I'm just saying I would have been happy with something half this size."

"I know, but I can't have it, Em. You deserve more."

"All I want is you," she whispered, stretching up on her tiptoes.

"You already have that."

Her legs wrapped around my waist when I picked her up, and we kissed in the middle of the winter-kissed park, the city rising behind us as snow fell from the sky around the igloo we stood in.

The touch of her tongue ignited stark hunger in me, and I kissed deeper, filling my hands with as much of her as I could. The cold metal of the ring on her finger brushed against my cheek and made me hum with satisfaction.

Pulling back, I snatched her hand so I could stare at the rock on her finger once again. "I love you."

"I love you too."

"You're gonna wear it, right?" I asked, worried she still might tell me to take it back. She was a sassy woman. I was gonna be on my toes for the rest of my life.

"I won't ever take it off," she vowed.

I kissed her again, all loud and noisy-like, and then I threw in a growl.

She laughed.

"Champagne," I said, setting her on her feet.

The sound of the cork popping off the bottle filled the little dome, and when I turned back with her glass, I noticed her staring toward the way we'd come.

"Where'd Pops go?"

I handed her the glass, then wrapped my arms around her from behind. "He's probably strolling with Finnegan. Wanted to give us some alone time."

Her head tilted in my direction. "He said he gave his blessing."

I made a sound.

She turned in the circle of my arms. "You asked him for permission?"

"I have impeccable manners. Of course I did."

Tears filled her eyes, and with a sound of distress, I pulled back to set aside both our glasses. "Hey, what's this?" I crooned, swiping at her cheeks.

"You included him. That means so much to me."

A soft sound fell between us when I kissed her softly. "I know, sweetheart. That's why I did it."

"Thank you."

Holding her face, I kissed her cheeks, her nose, her eyes, then gently brushed against her lips.

"Let's eat." I guided her to the table. "So we can go home, and I can eat what I really want," I whispered, biting her ear.

She laughed and plopped down in my lap instead of her chair. I was a much better seat than any old chair.

"Our first Christmas together, and it's already my favorite." She sighed, snuggling into my chest.

"Is that a challenge?" I quipped, leaning back to look down into her face.

"Boy!" she swore. "No, it's not, so don't even try."

I suppressed a snicker. I loved it when she sassed me.

"As long as I have you, then every Christmas will be perfect."

"Now how am I supposed to enjoy that sass when you follow it up with pretty words like that?" I complained.

She laughed.

My arms closed around her, hugging her tight. "You're right, though," I whispered. "Every Christmas is going to be perfect because we're going to be together."

19

GRINCH

PINE NEEDLES SCATTERED THE SIDEWALK, LOOKING LIKE rotten sprinkles against the snow, which looked no better having turned brown and dirty along the streets.

No one played normal, tolerable music anymore. Everywhere I went, the air was filled with earsplitting carols and jingling bells. Despise. Detest. Dislike!

The scent of roasting chestnuts? Stink. Stank. Stunk!

Everywhere I looked, people rushed around with packages, ribbons, and bows. From the moment I stepped onto the street, I counted down the minutes until I could retreat into my small apartment away from the noise, the people, and the cold.

If I could stop Christmas from coming, I would.

But not even county ordinances stopped the throat-clogging merriment. It was disgusting. The complete disregard for rules, safety, and the law!

"It's Christmastime!" they all purported. "'Tis all in

good fun. 'Tis the season!"

Blah. Belch. Blech.

"I've never seen Mr. Holly's tree stand so busy!" someone said, coming into the room.

I felt my upper lip curl in disgust.

"Pretty soon, they're going to be out of trees." Someone else chimed in.

"Good," I grumbled.

"Fletcher sure is drawing them in this year."

"He used to run around here stealing food, and now he's giving stuff away!"

"He's still the little criminal he always was," I snapped.

Heads turned in my direction. "You okay? You're looking a little green."

From the back, someone tacked on, "Green with envy!"

Laughter rang between my ears. Over the speakers, more Christmas music started to play.

"Ridiculous." I snarled. "Why would I be jealous?"

"It's not every day one of us finds out he's a rich heir and snags a handsome, princely boyfriend to go with his new shiny bank account."

"And instead of turning his back, he's here packing the sidewalks and handing out free trees!"

Bam! Everything on my desk rattled when I slammed my fist into it. My chair shot back, hitting the wall. "You all can sit here squabbling like raccoons over a full trashcan, going on about how wonderful he is now that he has money, but some of us have work to do."

I didn't bother to stop and put my coat on, just snagged it on my way to the door.

"Where you going?"

Of all the idiotic, dopey questions. I fumed.

"Crowd control!"

20

Fletcher

"MAKE SURE YOU GO SEE MY SISTER AT TANGLED STEMS. It's the flower shop the next block over. She has some ornaments that will look great on your tree," I called, waving to a family towing away a tree.

They waved back, and then the crowd shifted, and I couldn't see them anymore.

"Fletcher!" Mr. Holly bellowed from inside the little shack.

I went inside to see what he wanted. "Yes?"

He had a permanent frown on his face, so I never could quite tell if he was mad or if it was just the way he looked.

"I ain't never in all my years had my trees sell so fast. Pretty sure we'll be out of them completely by lunch tomorrow."

"Are you mad?"

"Hell no, boy! It's fantastic!"

Relief made me smile. "People sure do love your trees."

He made a rude sound. "We both know they're coming here to gawk at you, a richie working in the Grimms."

"I am not a richie."

His eyes turned squinty. "Then how you paying for all these trees you're giving away?"

My mouth opened. Closed. "I'm not giving them away. They're all being paid for."

"I might be old, but I'm not stupid. I know you're selling my trees for pennies and, in some cases, giving them away. Then you're putting the extra money in the drawer when you think I don't see."

"Everybody get moving!" someone yelled from out on the sidewalk. "This is loitering!"

"What in tarnation is going on now?" Mr. Holly wondered.

"I'll go see," I offered, taking the opportunity to get out of our conversation. Who cared if I was maybe giving trees away? It felt good.

Out on the sidewalk, I spotted Fig in full uniform a little ways down the sidewalk. "Gonna have to ask you to vacate the premises."

"I'm not loitering. I'm waiting in line to pay!" the woman he was facing exclaimed.

"You're blocking traffic."

"Shut the hell up, Fig! Go do some actual work and stop bothering everyone!" someone else in line yelled.

Fig's face darkened.

"Freaking rent-a-cop," someone grumbled.

It was nearly dark. The string lights overhead glowed down on everyone, and the night air was especially frigid. As I went toward Fig, I snuggled down into my coat a little farther, my fingers curled in on themselves inside the mittens Ethan gave me.

"Fig," I called. "Why are you trying to chase off customers?"

"Just doing my job."

"They're getting Christmas trees, not breaking the law."

Mr. Holly appeared, waving around a paper before pushing it into Fig's chest. "Now see here. I have a permit! I'm allowed to be selling my trees here, and these people are allowed to shop!"

Fig studied the paper as if he'd never seen something like it before, and we all knew he had.

Why is he being so difficult? It's like he hates Christmas. Or maybe he just hates me.

"This should be on display in your business." Fig sniffed, handing the paper back to Mr. Holly.

"Maybe I oughta staple it to your forehead!"

"Threatening an officer is against the law."

"He didn't mean it. He's just frustrated because you keep trying to kick us out," I told him.

"Grinch!" someone hollered.

Fig's mouth drew into a hard line.

"Fine. Keep crowding up the sidewalk and smelling up the place with your dead trees." Glancing back at the crowd, he said, "That's right. You're all waiting in line to purchase dead wood."

"Have you ever had a Christmas tree before?" I asked him quietly.

His mouth slapped shut, and he spun to face me.

"Have you?" I pressed.

"A long time ago," he said, stuffing his hands in his pockets.

I started to say something, but he cut me off. "I'll be

watching this place. One foul move, and I'll shut you down!"

He stalked away before I could say more, and I watched as he crossed the street, foot sloshing in a big pile of slush.

"Disgusting!" His yell carried on the wind, and I watched him shake his boot. It made him look like he was trying to kick a ghost.

Not much later, Ethan's white Mercedes slid to a stop at the sidewalk not far from the stand. I waved wildly even though he probably was busy shutting off the car, then spun to Mr. Holly.

The older man chuckled. "Go on, then. Get out of here."

"But don't you need help closing up later?"

"I've been running this stand since before you were born. I can handle it just fine," he snapped. Then softening his voice, he said, "You've done enough."

"See you tomorrow!" I said and headed toward the Mercedes.

Ethan was no longer inside the car. Instead, he was walking my way, looking just like the prince I always thought him to be, dressed in a long green coat with a high neck that framed out his sharp jaw. The second he saw me, he smiled, and butterflies took over my stomach.

"You didn't have to get out," I told him as a particularly bitter wind cut down the street. The temperature must have been dropping.

"Nonsense," he said, reaching out to cup his hand around the back of my neck and draw me forward. His fingers were warm, making me lean into them. "Where's your scarf?" he exclaimed, glancing down at my neck.

I shrugged, a little sheepish.

He sighed. "You gave it away, didn't you?"

I nodded. "Are you mad?"

Groaning, he pulled me into his chest, wrapping his arms around me. I breathed in deep, pressing closer. It always used to surprise me how openly affectionate Ethan was in public. He didn't ever seem to care who saw us or if anyone knew we were together. I wasn't surprised anymore, though. Now I just enjoyed it. I liked having someone love me that much.

"How could I be mad at you?" He spoke over my head.

Pulling away, he unwound the cashmere scarf around his neck to drape it around mine.

"This is too fancy!" I fussed, trying to take it off.

He made a rough sound. "Be a good boy."

I relented, and he finished tucking it into my coat.

"Don't worry," I told him, holding up my hands. "I would never give away these mittens you just gave me. Or the hat."

Smiling, he put his arm around me. "C'mon, we have to go."

Even though I told him not to a thousand times, he still went around to the passenger side and opened the door for me. Like I couldn't do it myself.

It was kinda nice, though, that he did it for me.

Before climbing in, I gazed across the street, stare finding Fig. He was huddled against a brick building, standing in the shadows away from all the Christmas lights.

"Fletch?" Ethan questioned when I didn't get in the car.

"I'll be right back," I told him, jogging across the street.

Fig straightened when he saw me approach. "Well, if it isn't Mr. Christmas himself."

"Why are you such a grinch?"

He jolted. "What?"

"Don't act surprised. You've been glowering at the tree stand since it opened."

He didn't say anything.

"Don't you like Christmas?"

"No!" He fumed.

"Why not?"

"It's none of your business why I don't like it. Not everyone has to."

I nodded. "I used to feel really lonely at Christmas. You remember her, right? My, ah, fake mom?"

Some of the anger left his face. "So? You think you're the only one with shitty parents?"

"No," I echoed, not hurt by his words. It was him that was hurt, and it made me feel kind of sad. Maybe because I understood why he was so grinchy. "I think lots of us have reasons to hate Christmas. Especially around here," I said, gazing up and down the street.

"What's your point?"

"Maybe you'd like Christmas better if you had someone to celebrate it with."

"I don't want to celebrate it. I want it to pass so we can go back to normal."

So he doesn't have to feel as lonely.

Reaching into my pocket, I pulled out one of Mr. Holly's tree stand cards and a pen. After scribbling an address on the back, I held it out.

"Tonight, any time after seven."

Gaze suspicious, he looked between me and the card, not moving to take it. "I don't want it."

I continued to hold it out anyway. "Take it. You could use a little social interaction."

"With who?"

I smiled. "Friends. Family."

He was no longer hostile and grumpy, maybe now just curious.

"Just take it. If you don't want to come, then don't. But if you do, I think you'll have a good time."

He took the card.

I beamed. "See you tonight!"

"I'm not coming!" he shouted after me.

I smiled at Ethan when I slid into the Mercedes.

"What was that about?" he asked, curious.

"Just trying to spread a little Christmas cheer."

"Did it work?" he asked dubiously.

"I guess we'll see."

21

NAT KING COLE CROONED THROUGH THE ENTIRE LOWER part of the townhouse courtesy of an old record player and the vinyl spinning around on top of it.

Pops had quite the collection of old records, and several of them were filled with Christmas songs. It brought me back to when I was little and Pops would twirl Mama around in front of the tree. They would laugh and drink eggnog. The house would smell like gingerbread, and they would still be dancing even after they sent me to bed.

Sometimes I would crack open my bedroom door and watch them slowly swaying close together with nothing but the lights from the tree illuminating the room.

I missed those days. Our more recent Christmases were just me and Pops, and it was wonderful but never quite the same. Maybe that was why I felt some nostalgia tonight, hearing the records as gingerbread baked in the oven and a huge bowl of eggnog sat on the island.

It wasn't just going to be me and Pops tonight. This Christmas, we were going to have an entire houseful. Setting aside the cookie I was icing, I glanced down at the ring on my finger. It was a beautiful stone, but what was more beautiful to me was the promise it held.

No more holidays with just me and Pops. Now there would be Ander and the rest of our family, and maybe someday we'd have a few kids of our own.

"Em!" Ander hollered as he entered the kitchen.

Boy just liked yelling my name like that. There could be no other reason why he did it every single day.

"Em!"

I made a sound and looked up. "You can see I'm right here."

Standing in the wide doorway between the kitchen and the living room, a slow smile spread over the lower half of his face, and he pointed up.

I groaned. "I'm about to throw that mistletoe in the trash!"

"Get over here and kiss me."

"I'm busy."

A harsh sound vibrated his throat. "Too busy to kiss your husband?"

"We aren't married yet."

He growled.

"You don't scare me, Ander Todd."

Storming across the room, he snatched me off my feet, tossing me over his shoulder like I was a sack of potatoes. "Ander!" I shrieked, smacking his back.

Ignoring my protests, he carried me back to the doorway, placing me on my feet. Anchoring his hands at my hips, he stepped closer, our bodies bumping together. "Look at that. You aren't so busy anymore."

My breath whooshed out when he jerked me flush against him, planting his feet wide to support my weight. His smoldering blue eyes locked on mine as he dipped his head to claim what he wanted.

A low grumble vibrated his lips as they moved restlessly over mine, clinging to mine in all the right places. Our mouths rubbed together in an intimate massage, saliva mingling as my fingers delved into the short hair at the back of his head. The trimmed beard on the lower half of his face was both silky and a little rough, one moment making me tingle and the next soothing over the place it just excited. Fingers dragging from his hair, I caressed his jaw, rubbing the pads of my fingers across the beard.

Grunting in satisfaction, he sucked my lower lip between his, tugging it out away from my face before gently letting go.

"You taste like gingerbread." His voice was gravelly and rough.

"Because I just ate one."

Our noses bumped when he kissed me again. Soft and sweet, just enough to leave me a little breathless. He left me like that, blinking like I was dumb under the mistletoe he insisted we hang.

Lip-smacking and *crunch, crunch, crunch* made me blink.

Gasping, I went over to snatch the cookie he'd just stolen out of his hands, but the freaking beast shoved the entire thing in his mouth.

"Are you for real?" I hollered. *Chomp, chomp.* A crumb fell from his lip. "When you choke, I'm gonna stand here and watch you die."

"No you wouldn't," he said around his mouthful, leaning in to fan his gingerbread breath all over my face. "You'd give me CPR."

I picked up a spatula I'd been using and whacked him with it. "I told you no cookies 'til everyone got here."

"Ow!" he hollered, snatching up another cookie and biting its head off.

I gasped.

"That's what you get for hitting me!" He shoved the rest into his mouth.

I raised the spatula over my head. "I'm about to hit you again."

Moving like the wrestler he was in college, he grabbed my wrist and somehow switched us around so I was pinned between him and the counter, the utensil pinned against my back between us.

"What are you gonna do if I like it?" he whispered in my ear.

Awareness tingled my scalp, and I arched into him, pushing my ass into his crotch. He purred low, pressing his lips against the side of my neck.

"Are you still chewing?" I demanded.

He laughed. The sound affected me just as much as his suggestive teasing, just in different ways. I wanted nothing more than for him to be happy.

But boy needed to keep his hands off the cookies.

"Ow!" he wailed when I slapped his fingers as he reached for another. "Em," he whined.

"Sorry, boo. You have to save some for everyone else."

He moved back just enough for me to be able to turn so we were facing each other. "Just one more?" he asked, batting those baby blues at me.

"That doesn't work on me."

He switched over to accusations. "But you ate one too!"

"That was different. I was taste-testing."

"Just one more?" His voice was soft, the slightly raspy tone always making my stomach flip. To punctuate the soft words, he lifted my left hand, drawing it up to press a kiss to the ring he'd put there not very long ago.

I sighed. "Fine. One more."

He smiled against my fingers.

"Spoiled ass," I muttered.

"Mmm," he said around another bite. "This your mama's recipe?"

"How'd you know?"

He shrugged. "All your favorite recipes are hers."

"She made these with me when I was little."

He took another, more civilized bite and chewed slowly. His eyes drifted shut, and he smiled softly. "When I eat it like this, it sort of feels like she's here with us right now. Like even though I never got to meet her, I kinda just did."

Oh, the sweetness. Mama would have loved him. Sniffling a little, I glanced at the tray of cookies. "Eat as many as you want, boo."

The doorbell rang, and I moved to answer it. He caught me around the waist, towing me back into his body. "Pops will get it."

The sound of voices floated into the kitchen, and I started forward again.

"Em."

I turned back.

"I love you."

Everything inside me softened. "I love you too, boo."

Grinning, he snagged another cookie off the counter and took my hand with his.

"You have cookie in your teeth." I sassed.

"I'm saving it for later." He sassed back.

Boy was too charming for his own good.

"Hi, guys!" Fletcher said the second we stepped into the room.

"Hey, Fletch," I said, going forward to hug him because he hugged everyone. I wasn't much of a hugger (except with Ander), but Fletcher was kind of the exception. After he hugged me, he went for Ander.

"The tree looks so good!" he exclaimed, going over to it. "Ethan, look how good it looks."

Ethan smiled indulgently. "You did a good job with the lights, Ander."

Ander groaned. "Uncooperative little buggers, they are."

I thought it was funny how his elitist upbringing popped out a little more when Ethan was in the room.

Before Pops could even come back into the room, the doorbell rang again. This time, Neo and Ivory came inside.

"Oh, it just looks lovely in here," Ivory remarked, looking around. "Emogen, you have an eye for design."

"Thanks, girl," I said.

"Emogen." Neo greeted me, holding out his hand and offering me an ornery grin. Laughing, I reached out, and we did the secret handshake we always used to do when he came to the Tower when V lived there.

"You still remember," he said, grinning.

"Like riding a bike."

Chuckling, he moved to Ivory to help her slip off her coat. Beneath it, she was wearing a satin red jumpsuit with a halter-style neck that tied into a large red bow at the side of her neck. Her black hair fell in loose waves over her shoulders, and the only jewelry she wore was a gold cuff bracelet around one wrist.

"You should sit down," Neo told her, taking her coat.

Ivory's blue eyes rolled. "I'm perfectly capable of standing."

"You look great," I told her, and she smiled.

"I was just thinking the same thing about you."

I glanced down at the silver sequin wrap dress I was wearing. "I'm probably covered in flour. I was just finishing up the cookies."

"Cookies!" Fletcher echoed.

Ethan laughed.

"Better go get one before Ander eats them all," I told him.

He and Ander went to help themselves.

Pops came in the room, followed by Earth who was carrying a smiling Virginia. "Merry Christmas!" she told the entire room.

She was dressed in a pair of sparkly gold pants and a white sweater with a big sparkly snowflake on the front. The fishtail braid her hair was done up in had snowflakes pinned into it instead of flowers.

More greetings went around.

Ethan excused himself to go grab her wheelchair from outside, and when he came back, it was with Beau, Daeshim, and the Cossgroves.

"We have a full house tonight!"

"Fletcher," Ethan called, "you have visitors."

A few seconds later, Fletcher appeared, a cookie in both hands. "Mom?" he said, eyes widening. "Dad?"

Samantha Cossgrove instantly dissolved into tears, turning to her husband who put his arm around her.

Fletcher seemed to shrink right before my eyes.

Ethan moved close, pulling him into his side immediately.

"What did I do?" Fletcher asked him.

Samantha cried harder.

"Family drama already," Daeshim drawled, glancing
around the room.

Earth grunted, carefully placing V on the couch.
Snort, who I didn't even know was here, jumped up on
the cushion beside her.

"Beer's in here," Ander called from behind Fletch.

"Thank God," Earth muttered, starting away. Then he
stopped and leaned over the back of the couch to V. "Do
you want something?"

"No, thank you."

He kissed her temple and disappeared, Beau and
Daeshim following after him. As soon as Ivory was
sitting by V, Neo followed.

"Ethan?" Fletcher asked, reaching out to grab the
front of his sweater.

"You called her mom, puppy," Ethan said, running a
hand down his back.

Fletcher's eyes widened. "I'm sorry!" he hurried to
say, rushing toward his parents. "I didn't mean to upset
you. It just kind of came out. I—"

Samantha grabbed him up in a crushing hug, stopping his words. "No, please don't apologize. I've waited
so long. I'm so happy."

Fletcher glanced at me over his mother's shoulder. I
smiled.

"So you aren't mad?"

"Good heavens, no, son." Henry Cossgrove spoke up.
"We are absolutely delighted. You can call us that
anytime you want."

"Are you sure?"

"Oh, yes," Samantha said, pulling back to look at him. "It's the best Christmas present ever, and knowing you just said it naturally, it means you really do see us as your parents."

Fletcher nodded, a small sound escaping him. It was all he had to do for Ethan to be there, stepping right up against his back.

"Would anyone like some eggnog?"

"Girlie, I've been waiting all day for a taste of that heaven," Pops declared, rubbing his hands together.

"That's quite a beautiful record player there. Do you have a collection of vinyl?" Henry asked him.

I nearly groaned. That was going to be a long conversation.

Samantha sat down with Ivory and V, and I went off into the kitchen for the nog.

On the way by, Ethan stopped me. "I hope it's okay the Cossgroves came. With it being their first Christmas with Fletcher, I didn't want to deny them this chance."

I patted his arm. "It's more than okay. I'm glad you invited them."

"Thank you."

"You can thank me by helping me serve the eggnog," I said, waving him into the kitchen.

Earth snorted. "That richie has never served anything a day in his life."

"That's not true!" Fletcher refuted. "He brings me coffee in bed all the time."

Beau groaned. "There is some information brothers don't need."

"I'll bring you coffee in bed, Fletcher," Daeshim quipped.

Ethan lunged for Daeshim, making me gasp. Ander

was there instantly, shoving me behind him and wrapping his arms around Ethan's waist to pull him back.

"I've had just about enough out of you," Ethan spat, pushing the sleeves up on his sweater.

"Should have let him hit him," Beau observed.

Fletch stepped in front of Ethan, laying a hand on his chest. "Don't be jealous, E. You're my only."

The tension drained out of Ethan's body, and Ander let him go, slapping him on the back. "Let's get a drink."

"Do you happen to have any scotch?" Ethan asked, still eyeing Daeshim.

"You're all getting eggnog, and if you insult it, I'll take it as slander against my mama and kick you out of the house," I declared, already filling cups.

"And I'll help her." Ander agreed.

Once everyone in the kitchen had a glass, I carried a tray out into the living room filled with some for everyone else.

Everyone gathered in the living room, the tree glimmering, the fireplace crackling with Pop's old-school music playing.

I glanced around at the many people who'd become my family and marveled a little at how much Ander changed my life. Glancing at him, pride swelled in my chest because he stood there without a hoodie, shoulders back, and head high. He was comfortable in this home and with all the people around us. He trusted them, and he didn't feel the need to hide.

"A Christmas toast," I said, raising my glass. Everyone did the same.

Except Earth. "Toasts are stupid."

Virginia elbowed him, and he raised his glass.

"My living room has never had so much family in it. And honestly, everyone, this house might be full, but my heart is even fuller. Thank you for becoming our family. For giving us a place to fit. Here's to the first of many memorable Christmases and all the times in between."

"And here's to us getting married!" Ander declared.

Gasps went around the room. Virginia started to clap.

"Married!" Ivory exclaimed. She jumped up to race forward. As she did, she tripped on her heels and pitched sideways. A strangled sound left Neo's throat as he rushed forward, catching her around the middle.

"How anyone can be so graceful and prone to life-threatening clumsiness, I will never understand," he muttered.

"Thank you for catching me," Ivory said.

His voice was gruff. "Be careful, princess," he said, setting her back on her feet.

The second he let go, she rushed over and hugged me. "Congratulations!" she declared. "Let me see the ring."

"I want to see too," Virginia exclaimed.

The next thing I knew, Virginia was beside Ivory, Earth holding her out like she was a rag doll.

"Someone's showing off his new muscles," Beau cracked.

Earth made a face like something smelled.

"I love it," Virginia exclaimed. "Oh, it's stunning!"

"Ander, you have impeccable taste," Ivory told him.

"Congratulations!" Virginia squealed, holding out her arms so she could hug me.

Earth sighed loudly behind us.

Virginia giggled. "I'm so happy for you."

"Thanks," I whispered.

Ethan lifted his glass, reminding us all I'd been about

to give a toast. "Congratulations to Ander and Emogen. May you have a lifetime of love."

"Here, here," everyone echoed.

People sipped the eggnog, and Ivory went back to where she left her glass, lifting it to her lips.

"No!" Neo roared, lunging up to knock the glass out of her hand.

It hit the coffee table and shattered, eggnog splashing everywhere.

Ivory shrieked, holding out her hands to look down at herself. "Oh no," she wailed.

Girl was a bit dramatic.

Grabbing her, Neo spun her around, patting her down. "What is it? Are you cut? Are you hurt? Are—"

"This will never come out. This outfit is satin," she wailed.

Neo nearly sagged to the floor with relief.

"Unbelievable," Earth muttered.

"Now no use in crying over spilled milk," Pops said, still sipping at his *milk*. "Just like Mariah used to make it," he told me.

"Who the hell put alcohol in that eggnog?" Neo roared.

Beside me, Ander stiffened.

I wrapped my hand around his wrist to calm him. "I did. It's the recipe."

"Why the hell didn't you say anything?" he hollered again.

A rumble echoed in Ander's chest. But I didn't need him to beast out. I could deal with Neo on my own.

"Well, considering you were just swigging beer in my kitchen, I didn't think you had a problem with alcohol."

"Yeah, me, not my kid." He punctuated his shout by stabbing a finger at Ivory's stomach.

A complete moment of shocked silence rippled through the room. Even the record player skipped a beat.

"Kid?" Beau echoed.

"Neo!" Ivory exclaimed. "That's not something you just yell. And this mess…" She stared sadly at the broken glass and nog-covered coffee table.

A low curse fell from his lips. Then he winced and glanced at the Cossgroves. "Apologies."

"I'm sorry, princess," Neo spoke softly, moving up to Ivory's side to slip his arm around her waist. "I didn't mean to just blurt it out."

"Ivory, are you pregnant?" Virginia said, eyes wide.

Her hand went to her stomach, a soft smile turning her face dreamy. "Surprise!"

Chaos erupted.

22

Neo

No one was more shocked to find out about the baby than me.

But a close second was probably Earth who sat still during all the chaos and congratulations. I would have thought he'd turned to stone if not for the way he would reach out and hold Virginia to help her keep her balance as she all but lost her mind over her new niece or nephew.

She was going to be the best aunt.

The second I was done cleaning up the eggnog I, ah, spilled all over the place, I glanced at him. He avoided my eyes. I was about to call him out, but Ivory made a sound, effectively stealing my attention. Even though we'd been together a while now, she still took my breath away. She still looked like she stepped right out of a storybook. And now? Now she was adding another chapter. A chapter that proved we somehow successfully blended our two worlds into one.

One perfect baby.

"You okay, sweetheart?" I murmured, sliding onto the couch beside her.

"Don't be silly. Of course I'm fine. My outfit is stained and you ruined the surprise, but *I'm* fine."

I palmed her stomach. "And how about this little misfit?"

Her face softened, her small hand covering mine. "The baby is fine."

Emogen appeared with a mug of hot tea, holding it out to Ivory. "Here, take this."

"Oh, thank you so much," Ivory said, graciously accepting the drink. "I'm so sorry for the trouble."

"You aren't causing any trouble. Neo is."

I made a rude noise.

"Where's the lie?" Emogen countered.

"Don't be teaching my baby all that sass," I told her.

She cackled.

"I'm so happy!" Fletcher announced. "Not only am I getting a niece or nephew, but I finally won't be the baby of the family anymore."

"Yes, you will," everyone replied at once. Even his parents.

"Oh, come on!" Fletcher exclaimed.

Daeshim opened his mouth.

"I wouldn't if I were you," Ethan said coolly, stopping whatever he would say.

Beau snickered.

"I daresay that the whole of Manhattan will be up in arms," Samantha announced.

"We don't want to tell anyone yet, except for our family, of course."

"I am so excited!" Virginia exclaimed again, making me smile. "I'm going to spoil him or her rotten."

Ivory smiled, eyes a little misty. "This baby is very lucky to have such a big family."

Leaning in, I pressed a kiss against her temple. I knew what having a big family meant to her, and I knew what having her own children meant as well. Even though I was pretty shocked and kind of scared, I was beyond thrilled I was the one giving her the family she always wanted.

But not just her family. Mine too.

For so long, it had been just me and V. But not anymore. Not since Earth offered me a place to stay.

Leaning in to Ivory's ear, I whispered, "I'll be right back."

Her eyes glanced toward Earth, then back to me, and she smiled.

I patted her nonexistent belly, knowing that soon, I would have something to rub. "Be good in there," I told the baby.

On my way by, I slapped Earth on the shoulder. "Let's get a beer."

I didn't glance around to see if he followed. I didn't hear him, but I knew that didn't mean he wasn't there. Instead, I fished two longnecks out of the fridge, popped the tops, and finally turned.

Earth was right there, staring at me with unblinking, unreadable black eyes. I held out the beer. He took it.

"You got a problem with Ivory being pregnant?" I decided not to mince words.

"Do you?"

Lowering the beer, I matched his intense stare with one of my own. "My baby is not a problem."

He grunted, nodding just barely. "Congratulations."

"You're cool?" I wanted to be sure. In truth, I wanted his approval. I almost needed him to be okay with this, so that little part of me that was still fucking scared shit-less would be okay too.

"Why wouldn't I be?"

"You don't like kids."

"I don't like adults either."

I cracked a smile. "Fair enough."

"She was really fucking happy," he said a moment later.

My mouth curved up, thinking at first he meant Ivory. But then I realized he was talking about my sister. "Yeah. Virginia always liked kids."

He frowned at the beer in his hand. "It's something I can't give her."

Ahh. *Is this happening right now? Is Earth actually opening up a little?*

"Can't or won't?" I challenged. Despite the little bit of awe I felt that he was willingly talking to me, I knew enough not to fuck it up or he'd never talk to me again.

"Both."

"She can't have kids anyway," I whispered, knowing it was my fault, feeling the pain of that pierce the deepest part of me.

Earth's eyes flared. "Yes, she can."

Shock rippled through me. "Don't play games like this."

"I don't ever play games when it comes to your sister. You know that."

I did know. Earth was a hard, dangerous man. But he loved my sister with every ounce of himself.

"Are you sure?" I asked, doubtful.

"As if I wouldn't be sure about anything having to do with V," he snapped.

"I-I didn't know."

He grunted. "You never asked."

"Asking my sister about her girl parts isn't exactly on my to-do list." I defended. *Plus, it was one more thing I'd have to hear her tell me I took away.*

"Well, I asked." He seemed pretty pleased with himself, and frankly, I didn't like knowing he knew about my sister's girl parts. "And she can have kids. It would be pretty safe."

Relief filled me, offering up a lightness I hadn't known I needed. "Wow," I said, digesting the information. Inwardly, I celebrated the fact I hadn't stolen her chance at motherhood.

Then I remembered his earlier words. I scowled. "You refuse to give her a baby?"

His voice was strained. "You know I can't do that."

Was that a trace of regret I heard in his tone?

"Did you tell her that?" I asked, my anger at him dissipating. I wasn't the only one with demons. And honestly, his were far worse than mine.

He gave a clipped nod.

"And she still chose you?"

For the briefest of moments, the walls Earth kept erected around him fell. I saw past all his hard edges, his defense mechanisms, and his pain. I got a glimpse of the man my sister likely knew.

"Yeah, she did," he replied, voice humble.

This was why, even when I tried, I couldn't hate him. I never would.

"Then I guess she wants you more than she wants kids."

His eyes whipped to mine. He hadn't been expecting that.

"If there's one thing I learned, one thing you actually

helped show me…" I began. "It's that my sister knows what she wants. She's strong and brave. And she has a big heart. So if she told you it was okay, then it's okay."

"I'm a selfish bastard," he whispered.

"Yeah." I grinned. "But I am too. I kept her from so much life because I was too scared to give it to her."

Earth said nothing, but I knew he was listening.

"You took her to see the Rockettes."

Earth scowled. "Some richie hit on her when I went to take a piss."

I laughed but sobered up too quick. "I never took her anywhere."

"You had your reasons," Earth replied.

"So I guess you can give her what I can't."

"And you can for me." He finished.

I nodded. "She'll get plenty of baby time with her niece or nephew. So will you."

Earth's eyes narrowed. "You trust me with your kid?"

I didn't bother to point out I'd let him sleep with my sister. "Yeah, Earth. I trust you with my kid."

"Fuck," he muttered and chugged some beer.

I suppressed a smile. "We good?"

"Let's never talk like this again."

I nodded. "But if you ever need to, I'll be here."

"Earth!" Virginia called from the other room.

Straightening, he went to the doorway, putting eyes on my sister. "What?" he bellowed. Clearly, she was okay.

"Bring me a cookie!"

"Get it yourself."

"My legs don't work!"

My mouth dropped open, but Earth just chuckled under his breath.

"She's a fucking menace. Just like you," he said, actual

fondness in his tone. Snatching a cookie off the island, he started toward the living room.

"I want one too!" Fletcher called.

"For fuck's sake," he muttered, coming back to grab another.

"What about me?" I cracked.

"Get bent."

I laughed.

Ding-dong!

"Are we expecting anyone else?" Ander asked Emogen.

She shook her head, the sparkly red clips in her hair catching the light. "I'll see who it is."

Ander snatched her around the waist, towing her back. "Like hell."

"I think I know who it is," Fletcher said, surprising us all.

"You invited someone?" I asked.

"Is that okay?" he asked, turning to Ethan.

"So that's what that was about," he mused.

"He's lonely," Fletcher said.

Curiosity made me look toward the door.

"Why are you asking Ethan if it's okay? This isn't his house," Earth intoned.

Fletcher grimaced. "Is it okay, Ander?"

"Sure."

"I'll answer it, then," Fletch said, disappearing into the foyer.

I heard Fletcher talking and then the low hum of another voice. A voice that was kind of familiar. Seconds later, Fletcher appeared, smiling from ear to ear. A moment later, Fig appeared over his shoulder.

We all stared in shock.

"What the hell is he doing here?" Earth demanded, finally breaking the stunned silence.

Fig bristled, but Fletcher remained calm. "I invited him."

"He's arrested you every chance he got." Earth fumed.

"Ivory too." I reminded everyone.

"You're going to allow this?" Earth demanded toward Ethan.

Ethan made a face. "Oh, now you think I'm useful?"

"Fig is like us. A misfit. And he doesn't have any family or even a Christmas tree at home. No one should be alone at Christmas. So I invited him. We always have room for more family."

"What a kind heart you have, son." Samantha sniffled.

"Well, please come in, Officer Fig," Ivory said, gracefully unfolding from the sofa. She looked every ounce the powerful heiress she was, but she wasn't cold. She was warm. "Go stand by the fireplace and warm your hands. It's so cold out tonight."

"Would you like some eggnog? It's my mama's recipe."

"Best eggnog you'll ever have," Pops declared.

"Never thought I'd see the day when I'd be drinking with a cop," Daeshim quipped.

"Merry Christmas, Fig," Beau called. "Come on in and tell us the latest Grimms gossip."

"What makes you think I know any?" Fig asked. I could tell he was still awkward and grouchy, but he moved toward the fireplace.

I knew the guy was annoying as hell and a pain in the ass, but I never realized he didn't have any family.

"You know everything going on in the Grimms. It's what you do," I answered.

Emogen appeared with some eggnog, handing it over to him.

Ander handed him a cookie. "If you don't eat that, I will."

"Honestly, Ander!" Emogen scolded.

Fletcher went and sat in Ethan's lap. "Fig, Ivory and Neo are going to have a baby!" he told him.

Fig's eyes widened. "Really?"

Ivory nodded.

"Congratulations," he said, sipping the drink. Afterward, he glanced down. "What is this again?"

"Why?" Emogen's eyes narrowed.

"It's the best thing I've ever had!" he declared.

"Oh, well, in that case…" Em began telling him all about the eggnog.

I scooped up Ivory and cuddled her and my growing baby in my lap. Another old song started playing as the fire popped and hissed. Outside, the cold wind howled, but inside?

We misfits were merry.

23

GRINCH

I CAME TO STEAL AWAY THEIR JOY. I CAME TO MAKE them see.

To truly make them understand how rotten Christmas can be.

I stood on the porch, glaring at the lights, wreath, and snow.

Then from inside, I heard their warm laughter, and my heart started to grow.

Instead of pounding on the wooden door, I politely rang the bell.

When it opened up and they invited me in, I expected Christmas hell.

The people I was the worst to smiled and welcomed me in.

And now here I stood among all the merry misfits, and I couldn't help but grin.

In the end, I couldn't steal their joy, and it was them who made me see.

Maybe Christmas wasn't so terrible.

Perhaps tonight, Christmas was bearable.

24

Christmas morning…

EARTH

"IT'S SNOWING!" VIRGINIA EXCLAIMED. "EARTH! COME see!"

"I've seen the snow before," I told her, staring at the coffeemaker, willing it to hurry up.

Who wakes up this early in the morning? My girl. And not just on Christmas either. Every day. She was a total morning person, and it was just one more thing about her I would never understand.

"Earth!"

Leaving behind the coffeepot, I went into the living room where she was yelling like it wasn't the ass crack of dawn. "Who needs a rooster when I have you?" I grumped.

She didn't even turn around, too enthralled with the snow we'd seen a million times. My heart tumbled a bit seeing her there, framed by the window, staring out. She had a giant red Santa hat on her head, the white fur trim sticking out everywhere.

Her hair, which still wasn't as long as it used to be, hung over her shoulders like spun gold.

Still staring at the big white flakes, she held her arm out, palm up. "Come see."

"Something special about this snow?" I asked, walking closer.

"It's Christmas snow."

I made a sound. She was ridiculous.

Her face turned up. The white puffball on the end of the hat nearly bumped her cheek, and it was so big it nearly covered her eyes.

Chuckling, I adjusted it so I could see more of her.

She held her arms up, and I swung her up into mine, the hat tickling my neck when she laid her head on my shoulder.

"Merry Christmas, Earth."

"Merry Christmas, sweetheart."

Snort made a sound, and I looked down. "What in the hell did you do to my dog?" I demanded.

"I didn't do anything to him!" V declared. "He likes it."

She'd put antlers on him. And a Christmas sweater. "For shit's sake," I muttered.

"Don't you curse at me!"

Snort barked.

"Tell him, Snort."

"You're ganging up on me now?"

She smiled sweetly. That was never a good sign. "I got you a hat too."

"No."

"But then we'll match."

"Forget it." I denied again. Carrying her to the couch, I sat her in the center, noting her bare feet. Reaching down, I wrapped my hand around one. "Your feet are freezing!"

She shrugged.

I flipped a blanket over her lower half, covering her icy feet. Going over to the lighted tree, I grabbed a crudely wrapped box and brought it to her. "Here."

Her eyes ignited. My heart turned over again.

"What's this?"

"A Christmas present."

"For me?"

"Who else would it be for?"

Grabbing it, she hugged it against her chest. "I love it!"

"You haven't even opened it," I told her, going back into the kitchen for coffee. It was finally done brewing. I grabbed a mug shaped like Santa from beside the pot and poured. "Sweetheart, you want coffee?"

"Yes, please." A beat of silence. "Make sure you use the Christmas mugs!"

"I'd never dream of not using them," I said, adding creamer to her coffee.

It reminded me of Fletcher. I wondered if he was awake yet. He probably was letting Ethan sleep in. Assholes.

"Here, baby," I said, holding her mug over the back of the couch.

"Mmm," she said, leaving the gift in her lap to grab the coffee with both hands. She smiled brightly at me, and her hat slid over her eyes again.

I couldn't help it. I smiled and then fixed it while she was sipping the coffee. "Why didn't you open it yet?"

"I can't open it without you."

I started to sit down.

"No!" she yelled.

"Now what?" I demanded.

"Get one of yours too." She pointed to the gifts under the tree.

"You first." I decided, sitting down and lifting the mug to my lips.

She pulled a Santa hat that matched hers from under one of the cushions. I nearly spit the coffee all over my shirt.

"I said no."

Her lower lip jutted out.

I mean, really. I was a hard man. A killer. But not even I could withstand her hopeful stare and pouty mouth as she sat on the couch under a blanket with her legs out in front of her and that damn hat on her head. And hell, her hand looked so small wrapped around that stupid mug.

"Fine," I grumbled, setting aside my coffee and leaning over.

Squealing a little beneath her breath, she tugged the hat over my hair, adjusting it until she was satisfied. It wasn't nearly as big on me as it was on her.

"Perfect!" she announced. "You look so cute."

"I'm not cute."

"You are to me," she sang and blew me a kiss.

I love her so much.

"We need a picture," she said, pulling out her cell phone, which was also in the cushions.

"What the hell else are you hiding in there?" I wanted to know.

"You hold the phone because your arm is longer."

My upper lip curled.

"Snort!" She beckoned, and the dog leaped onto the couch, walked over my lap, and poked me in the eye with his antler.

"Be careful." I warned the dog as he plopped himself on her lap. I knew she didn't care, but I sure as hell did. He could hurt her without her even knowing.

Giggling, she held out her arm for me. Muttering, I squeezed in.

"Your mug too!"

"I can't believe I'm doing this."

We took several selfies, all featuring us in these hats, the dog in antlers, and two giant Santa mugs.

"Can I please drink my coffee now?"

She nodded, and I pulled her into my lap, draping the blanket over us both. Snort moved off to lie on his bed, and I sipped my coffee while looking at the fire going in the fireplace. It was gas and only required a flip of a switch to turn it on.

"Come on." I nudged the gift at her. "Open it up."

Still snuggled into my lap, she ripped the red paper off the brown box and lifted the lid.

"Oh!" she exclaimed, reaching inside and pulling out the tall slipper boots. They were white and made of material that frankly looked like a bath mat to me, but it was soft. "They're so beautiful!" she said, pulling one up to rub it on her cheek. "And so soft."

See? She liked soft shit.

"The inside is fur!"

"I'm tired of your feet always being cold." She opened her mouth, but I cut her off. "I don't care if you can't feel it if they're cold. I don't like it."

Her face softened, and she hugged me, the discarded paper crinkling between us. "I love them."

Her ass wiggled around a whole lot in my lap as she

tugged them on, and I thought about pushing her into the cushions and doing things Santa would not approve of.

Knock, knock, knock!

V straightened. "Who could that be?"

"You have a delivery scheduled?"

Her nose wrinkled. "On Christmas Day? No way. People should be home, not delivering things."

Knock, knock, knock!

Shifting her onto the couch, I couldn't help but notice the way the fuzzy-looking boots swallowed up all of her lower legs. *Cute.*

There was more knocking, and Snort barked.

"I'm coming!" I yelled, undoing all the locks to yank open the door. "What in the—"

"Merry Christmas!" Fletcher exclaimed. Ethan stood right behind him, half smiling, half grimacing.

"Fletch?" I echoed, surprised. "What are you doing here?"

Fletcher's brows drew together slightly. "It's Christmas. You make pancakes every Christmas."

A rush of emotion caught me off guard. "You came for pancakes?"

Fletcher shrugged. "It's tradition."

"We brought presents," Ethan said, holding up an armful of bags.

I stared at them both, not saying anything.

"Was I not supposed to come?" Fletcher finally asked, a little worry in his tone.

I'd thought everything would be different this year. I didn't expect him to come... to think of the pancakes.

"Of course you were supposed to come," I finally said. Stepping back, I made room for them to come inside. "Get in here."

True to form, Fletcher hugged me on his way in. "Merry Christmas, Earth!"

"Merry Christmas," I said, allaying my gruff tone.

"Merry Christmas, Virginia," he called, moving off into the living room.

"Nice hat," Ethan said with a smirk.

"She probably has one hidden in the couch for you too."

That sobered him up real quick. "I was going to call, but I didn't want Fletcher to think he couldn't just show up."

I nodded. "You don't need to call. You guys are always welcome here."

"He said it wouldn't feel like Christmas without your pancakes."

"They aren't even that good," I said, feeling a lump form in my throat.

Ethan slapped me on the shoulder. "Well, they have to be better than the cookies I tried to make him."

"E! Come put the presents under the tree," Fletcher called.

As I was shutting the front door, a hand slapped into the wood on the other side. Without thought, my hand shot out through the slim opening, grabbing the arm in a punishing grip.

"Ow!" someone yelled. "It's me!"

"Neo?" I said, pulling open the door.

He was standing there scowling, rubbing his wrist. Ivory stood beside him. She looked very put-together for as early as it was. "You're lucky it was me and not her you grabbed."

I shrugged.

"What are you doing here?"

"It's Christmas," they both said as if it were obvious.

Am I the only one who didn't expect this?

I motioned for them to come inside. Virginia called out for her brother, and Ivory hugged me on her way in.

"He treating you okay?" I asked, giving her a gentle squeeze.

"Of course. But fair warning, he's even more protective now," she said, hand sliding over her flat stomach.

I still couldn't wrap my head around the fact that there was a kid in there.

When all I did was stand there and stare, she reached for my hand. "Do you want to feel?"

"Why? Does it feel different?"

"Not yet."

"Then why would I want to feel?"

"'Cause it's your niece or nephew."

I think this hat was making me emotional. V did something to it.

"Maybe later," I said.

She smiled. "Okay."

"Go sit down. You should rest."

She rolled her eyes. "You sound like Neo."

"He's right."

A groan ripped from her.

"Princess!" Neo exclaimed, appearing so fast even I was surprised. "What the hell did you do to her?" he demanded.

"I told you," Ivory whispered loudly.

Nine months of this? God help me. Turning my eyes to Neo, I said, "I told her to sit down."

He grunted. "I keep telling her that."

Instead of waiting for her to listen—which would never happen—he swept her up and carried her to the couch, putting her down beside V.

"Are we late?" Beau asked, stepping in from the hallway. Daeshim was steps behind him. They were both carrying presents too.

"Hi, guys!" Fletcher called from beside the tree.

"Nice hat," Daeshim cracked.

I gave him the finger.

"Please tell me there's coffee," Beau said, already heading for the kitchen.

"Make me some too," Daeshim called.

"Screw off!"

"It's Christmas!" Ivory gasped.

"Sorry," Beau muttered.

"You two still fighting?" I asked my brother.

"Just leave it alone," Daeshim said quietly. Something about that answer made the hair on the back of my neck stand on end.

I turned to follow him, but Ander, Emogen, and her Pops walked in.

"The gang's all here!" Fletcher called.

Emogen took one look at me and burst out laughing. "Should I call you Santa now?" she asked on her way to the tree with an armful of presents.

"Funny," I muttered.

"Earth, thanks for letting me tag along with my daughter and son. Nice place you have here."

I shut the door, doing up the locks. "You're family too and welcome here anytime," I said, turning around to look at him and Ander. "Hope you like pancakes."

"Pops, come look at Snort!" Emogen called.

I sighed. "That poor dog."

Ander laughed beneath his breath.

"Ethan call you?" I quietly asked him when we were alone.

Ander made a sound of agreement. "Said it's tradition."

My eyes strayed toward Virginia who was sitting in the center of the chaos, laughing. Then they moved to Fletcher who was beside her, doing the same. Something a hell of a lot like happiness moved through me.

Or maybe it was Christmas spirit.

Maybe in Ethan's quest to give Fletcher the things he never had, he somehow gave it to the rest of us too. As if sensing my thoughts, Ethan glanced up and smiled.

I smiled back. I told you. This damn hat is making me crazy.

I clapped Ander on the shoulder. "It's definitely tradition. A misfit tradition."

"It's kinda nice," Ander echoed.

"Yeah," I replied.

"Earth!" Virginia yelled. "Come open your presents."

"Neo didn't bring any." Daeshim heckled.

"They're in the car," he argued. "I had to help Ivory up the stairs."

"Yes, because heaven forbid I walk on my own," she declared.

"Just send Daeshim down to get them. He's not doing anything anyway," Beau quipped, drinking coffee out of a mug shaped like an elf. I had no idea where it had come from.

V probably had it hidden in the couch.

"No bickering on Christmas," Fletcher announced.

"Sorry, Fletch," Daeshim told him. "I didn't mean to upset you."

Ethan's face darkened but then cleared when Fletcher plopped down in his lap and kissed his cheek.

I scooped up V and sat down with her in my lap, and around us, Christmas chaos ensued.

And we all celebrated… Merrily Ever After.

AUTHOR'S NOTE

Once upon a time... a Christmas tale was written by coffee, Advil, and sleepless nights.

I knew I wanted to write a Christmas-themed novella for the misfits when I was first writing *Prince*. The moment Fletcher mentioned how he worked at the tree stand in the Grimms and loved it, I knew I wanted to write about it. I really wanted to be here for Fletcher and Ethan's first Christmas together, for Fletcher to be with his family and have the holiday he was denied as a child.

As I continued working on the series after *Prince*, my love for the entire family really grew. Each couple is different and unique, but they all still sort of fit, and I wanted to see how they would all do Christmas.

The idea of writing "dates" for each couple and some family time in between was something that really appealed to me because we could see them all but still get a little one-on-one time. As passionate as I felt about writing *Merry Misfits*, I have to say it was actually quite challenging. I got so in my head for this. Is it too much?

Is it not enough? Is one couple getting more attention (ahem, looking at you Ethan and Fletch, lol)? Is it too fluffy? Is the sex with tinsel too much...? Ha. Round and round my thoughts went. I struggled a bit getting started, then I basically skipped around to the couples who spoke to me the loudest.

It's easy to say, "Oh, it's just a holiday novella. I can bang this out." But dear lord, doing it is a whole other thing. Basically, the second I sent *Beast* off to editing, I had a few days of "downtime," which consisted of doing a bunch of other behind-the-scenes work, and then I had to get going on this. I was on a TIGHT deadline. I told myself I was crazy for taking this on after finishing a 112k-word novel (*Beast*), but I just wanted this so much. And since it's a holiday-themed novella (frankly, I think some would actually consider this a novel, lol), it had to be released around the holidays.

So basically, I dove in and got to work. I wrote this in under a month, but as Neo would say... One star. Do not recommend. Lol. I burned the midnight oil on this one way more than once. It came out a little differently than I expected, but I'm happy with it because I let the family be the guide. And about the family... How much bigger are they going to get? There are so many people to consider in these scenes, and when they are all together, it's frankly like putting a puzzle together. It's absolutely a challenge. But I've come to learn I really have this deep passion for this series. I'm not really sure how that came to be, but I do ponder it often. It's this deep passion that really keeps me going with them because this has been probably the hardest series I've ever written (to date).

Also, I really wanted to write this for you. For all the support you show this series and these characters. I wanted to write something to make you feel like you maybe spent some time in NYC at Christmas and felt a little bit of warmth in your heart. At the very least, I hope it made you smile.

Merry Misfits closes out my year of publishing in 2021, and though it started out kinda precarious, I'm really proud to say I pulled out four books this year—which is better than I did in 2020. I am excited to see what next year brings and hope you will stick around for that journey. Who else is ready for Beau? I have a feeling his book is going to be difficult with a capital D.

Happy holidays and best wishes in the New Year. See you next book!

~XOXO~
Cambria

ABOUT CAMBRIA HEBERT

Cambria Hebert is a bestselling novelist of more than
fifty titles. She went to college for a bachelor's degree,
couldn't pick a major, and ended up with a degree in
cosmetology. So rest assured her characters will always
have good hair.

Besides writing, Cambria loves a pumpkin spice latte,
staying up late, sleeping in, and watching K drama until
her eyes won't stay open. She considers math human
torture and has an irrational fear of chickens (yes,
chickens). You can often find her running on the
treadmill (she'd rather be eating a donut), painting her
toenails (because she bites her fingernails), or walking
her chihuahuas (the real bosses of the house).

Cambria has written in many genres, including new
adult, sports romance, male/male romance, sci-fi,
thriller, suspense, contemporary romance, and young
adult. Many of her titles have been translated into
foreign languages and have been the recipients of
multiple awards.

Awards Cambria has received include:

Author of the Year 2016 (UtopiaCon 2016)
The Hashtag Series: Best Contemporary Series of 2015
(UtopiaCon 2015)
#Nerd: Best Contemporary Book Cover of 2015
(UtopiaCon 2015)
Romeo from the Hashtag Series: Best Contemporary
Lead (UtopiaCon 2015)
#Nerd: Top 50 Summer Reads (Buzzfeed.com 2015)
The Hashtag Series: Best Contemporary Series of 2016
(UtopiaCon 2016)
#NERD Book Trailer: Best Book Trailer of 2016
(UtopiaCon 2016)
#Nerd Book Trailer: Top 50 Most Cinematic Book
Trailers of All Time (film-14.com)
#Nerd: Book Most Wanted to be Adapted to Screen:
(2018)
Amnesia: Mystery Book of the Year (2018)

Cambria Hebert owns and operates Cambria Hebert
Books, LLC.
You can find out more about Cambria and her titles by
visiting her website:
http://www.cambriahebert.com
Stay up to date on all of Cambria's new releases and
more by signing up for her newsletter:
http://eepurl.com/bUL5_5

ALSO BY CAMBRIA HEBERT

The Heven & Hell series

The Death Escorts series

The Take It Off Series

The Hashtag Series

The GearShark Series

The Amnesia Duet

The Public Enemy Series

The BearPaw Resort Series

The House of Misfits Series

Westbrook Elite Series

Standalone Titles:

Moth To A Flame

Mr. Fantasy

Distant Desires

Maneater

Blank

Whiteout

Check out all these and more here:

https://books2read.com/ap/RQDG6x/Cambria-Hebert